# Mama

Richard Anderson's n̲ you on a roller coaster ride with all the twists and turns you don't see coming. You want to look away, yet you find yourself peeking around each corner.

Anderson introduces us to two radically different main characters, each on his own restless journey with no end in sight. But then, they stumble upon the same path, and it leads them to unexpected discoveries that change everything.

**Helen Stine, Author of the award-winning novel, *The Truthful Story***

*Mamas' Boys* by Richard Allen Anderson is an emotional tale of two polar opposite protagonists whose worlds collide. You keep wondering where each of the book's characters' journeys will lead them.

Richard has crafted an exciting novel filled with surprises that will keep you guessing until the end.

**Stephanie Baldi, Author of The Sicario Files Trilogy, Nominated for Georgia Author of the Year**

(Even I didn't know where *Mamas' Boys* would end until the characters told me.)

**Richard Allen Anderson**

# Books by Richard Allen Anderson

**Vabella Publishing, 2013-2023:**

*The Adventures of Diggerydoo and Taller Too*
Illustrated for Children, 2016

*Taradiddle and Cookie Crumbs*
tales of Love, Mystery and Adventure, 2019

*for the Good Times, a love story*
Memoir, 2021

*Family Album*
A family history and memoir, 2022

Poetry Collections:
*Patchwork Poems*, 2023
*Winter Weeds*, 2019
*Potholes in Memory Lane*, 2016
*Another Season Spent*, 2013

**Dancing Crows Press, 2024**
*Mamas' Boys*
A Novel 2024

www.amazon.com/author/richardallenanderson

# RICHARD ALLEN ANDERSON

# MAMAS' BOYS

Text Copyright © 2024 Richard Allen Anderson

This novel is a work of fiction. Names, characters, businesses, organizations, places, events, and incidents are the product of the author's imagination or are used fictionally. Any resemblance of actual persons, living or dead, events, or locales is entirely coincidental.

ISBN 978-1-951543-32-7

Library of Congress Control Number: 2024916826

DANCING CROWS
PRESS

Printed in The United States of America

# Dedication

For Dolly
She made me do it

Fate, show thy force;
Ourselves we do not owe;
What is decreed must be,
And be this so.

—William Shakespeare, Twelfth Night

Accept the things to which fate binds you,
and love the people with whom fate brings you together, but do so with all your heart,

—Marcus Aurelius, Meditations

Destiny is no matter of chance. It is a matter of choice. It is not a thing to be waited for, it is a thing to be achieved.

—William Jennings Bryan

## Chance and Choice—Choice and Chance

As humans, we exert free will—making choices, accepting and rejecting. We believe therefore we hold destiny in our own hands and minds.

Yet all our innate predilections are handed down in our genes from known and unknown generations. And choices must be made between one thing and another placed in our paths by mere chance, pure luck or bad fortune.

There are rare times when two souls, two personalities acquire an immediate affinity for each other without consciously exerting the power of choice. Some have attempted to explain this phenomenon. Others merely accept the miracle.

This is an enigma, yet an undeniable force that draws some humans together and repels others. It is a spiritual essence, not controlled by intellect, but irresistible. Thus are our destinies formed and our fates sealed.

Richard Allen Anderson
September, 2024

| | |
|---|---|
| Nora | 1 |
| Mory | 4 |
| Bowie | 8 |
| Big John | 13 |
| Billy the Kid | 20 |
| Selena, Isabella, and Polo | 28 |
| The Double U | 33 |
| Lee Roy Johnson | 43 |
| Morgan Morel | 50 |
| Uncle Emile | 56 |
| Esther Morel | 62 |
| Hermit | 71 |
| Son of Satan | 78 |
| Denise | 84 |
| Julia | 92 |
| MacArthur | 100 |
| Cactus Hills P.D. | 108 |
| Monster | 115 |
| Rhonda & Rose | 121 |
| The TruFont Hotel | 127 |
| Detective Morel | 132 |
| Mamas' Boys | 139 |
| Mario & Mateo | 146 |
| Friends & Lovers | 150 |
| Coconspirators | 161 |
| Unwelcome Suspicions | 165 |
| Confrontations | 169 |
| Return to Reality | 173 |
| Et cetera | 176 |

# MAMAS' BOYS

# Chapter 1
# Nora

Nora Masters sat at her bedroom vanity, humming and singing along to some of her favorite gospel songs, *Wings of the Dove, I'll Fly Away, Softly and Gently.* Busy making up her face, she watched her eight-year-old son enter the room holding out his school book and heard him plead, "Mama, I need help. I don't get this stuff."

But Nora was in a hurry now. "Read the book again, Bows. It'll come to you."

"Mama, please, I really don't get it!"

*He used to be such a sweet little boy. Never a problem. Not now.*

"Damn it, Bowie! Would you stop! Don't you see I am busy with my hair and nails?"

She saw the boy shuffle from the room, head hung low. She knew he would not cry and laughed with relief when she heard the book slam against the wall of his room and thud to the floor. *Little shit. Get over it. You'll be fine.*

She turned back to the vanity mirror and ran a brush through her shoulder-length auburn hair. *Not much time to lose.* She hurriedly applied eye shadow, then bright red lipstick. Satisfied at last, she rose and quickly turned to her closet to select a dress for her date tonight.

*Can't still be here when Mory gets home.*

Dressed, she glanced at the mirror, smoothed the glossy fabric over her hips, gathered up her purse, and hurried into the kitchen, where the boy sat at the table, holding his head in his hands.

Bowie Masters stared at the open book page until it blurred and went blank. He watched his mother rush into the room. He pretended to study until she nudged his shoulder and handed him a scribbled note. "Here's my note, read it now."

*Heat up the tuna casserole in the fridge when your father comes home.*

*I will be out late.*

"Now you've got my note, Bows. No excuse to forget again and get your father all upset with me."

Even before the note, her brightly flowered dress and painted face had told him she would be leaving, leaving him alone again. He hated that face as much as he loved his mother.

"Mama, please." He rose to embrace her. Maybe this once she would change her mind and stay at home.

Nora Masters pushed her son away. "Bows, don't!" She knew he hated that nickname. "You'll mess me up with your huggin' and kissin'. Now be good and do your homework." She hurried to the door and left without a backward glance.

Alone, Bowie pulled the dish of leftovers from the refrigerator and emptied its contents onto the kitchen floor. He dropped his mother's note and mashed it into the mess with his foot. He left a trail of tuna footprints leading to his bedroom, wanting to sleep before his father returned, drunk or sober. Sleep might take away the pain that invaded his young head.

"Fuck you," he cried, "fuck you," and punched the pillow. "Fuck you. Fuck you!" as hot tears fell from his eyes.

~~~

When Nora did not come home on the morning of Bowie's tenth birthday, he pounded and shook his father until he awoke. "Where's Mama? Where's my mama?"

"Damned if I know or care," his father replied, bleary-eyed, not bothering to look at his distraught son.

Nora had not bothered to leave a note when she finally left Morris Masters for the pleasure of another man. What could she say really? For all her dreams of glamour, life with him and the boy was just too mundane to bear.

After the tenth day of her absence, Bowie stopped asking and did not speak to his father of his mother again. Thoughts of her abandonment were too painful. His emotions raged from resentment to unbearable sorrow while he attempted to bury her memory deep in his subconscious.

# Chapter 2
# Mory

Morris Masters was a small man in almost every way except for his ego and disproportionately large manhood. Since graduating from high school, he had worked second shift at Union Fabricating and Converting, an automaton feeding metal and plastic sheets into various machines that bent, punctured, folded and transformed them into a variety of products for military or domestic use. Except to remember to keep the fingers on his hands, there was little to occupy his mind, which often wandered into romantic fantasies with women his mind fabricated.

The plant managers liked him. He punched in on time, whistled while he worked, and punched out with a smile. Never a problem.

After almost two years on the job, Morris met Nora Hembein, the pretty new clerk in accounts and records, when he stopped by the office with a question about his Labor Day overtime pay.

The young woman shot him a quick, size-up glance, as cold as yesterday's gravy. "What can I do for you?" Morris thought, Jesus, what a body ... what a set.

He confided to Hank, his one good buddy. "I am going to ask Nora out ... you know, the looker in the office."

Hank laughed at him. "She's out every night with a different guy. You ain't got—"

"You'll see. Bet you a sawbuck."

Three weeks later, Hank forked over a ten spot to a grinning Morris Masters and listened to his tale of triumph.

"I spent half a week's pay for tickets to the US Festival in San Bernardino last Monday. Memorial Day. Seemed like she was about to laugh in my face until I showed her the tickets ... David Bowie headlined it, Rock Band Day. That new group, U2, played too, and others."

Masters' face shone in happy reverie. "We left here early. Got there by noon ... three-hour drive. It was massive, man. People sprawled all over the park. She loved it all, Stevie Nicks, The Pretenders ... but especially David Bowie. It went on for hours."

Hank turned to leave. "Good for, you, little man."

"Wait, there's more." Mory pulled Hank closer. "It was late. We were starving. This little motel ... The Moonglow ... had a bar and restaurant. Italian. Played Deano and Sinatra, Frankie Vallie, all the time we finished our pasta and chianti ... lotsa chianti."

"Great, Mory, great. So, did you get anything for your money?"

"We were both feeling the wine. I told her I couldn't finish the drive home, so she says, 'This is a motel, isn't it?'" Mory broke into a grin that almost split his face. "So we checked in. I was all over her. Finally, she says, 'Okay, sucker, go for it. This is your lucky night.'"

On Tuesday, Mory applied for and was granted first shift work in the shop. He needed to see his conquest regularly. At the first chirp of the noon whistle, he sprinted with some small gift in hand from the manufacturing floor to the office breakroom. "Guess what I brought you today, baby?"

Nora acknowledged Mory's presence by silently holding out her hands to accept his gift. She granted him a small smile in exchange for each day's offering—flowers or sweets or some small trinket. But Nora never accepted his pleas for a second date.

Then, one day, she whispered in his ear, "I'm pregnant."

Morris and Nora were married by a Justice of the Peace on a cold, dark December afternoon, with Mory standing as proud and tall as he had ever been. Nora, detached and dreamy, her baby bump barely showing, was pulled, surprised, from her trance by the JP asking, "Will you, Nora, take this man?"

"Yeah, sure, go for it."

The JP exhaled. "Please answer with 'I do or I will.'"

Driving home after the ceremony, Nora informed Mory, "I was thinking back there about the baby. A name. I'm going to name him Bowie. And he will learn to play guitar. Yeah, we'll call the baby Bowie." And she fell silent again.

When Nora left Mory and her young son ten years later to fend for themselves, Mory seemed to shrink even smaller than his paunchy five foot five and one-half inches. The booze that had made the sham marriage bearable for the past years now anesthetized most of his waking hours.

Young Bowie returned from a day at school to find his father sprawled on the couch. A Ten High Kentucky Bourbon bottle lay on its side on the floor, not quite empty. The television cast varying shadows across the darkened room. Bowie stepped across the litter of old newspapers, dirty dishes, and random articles of clothing to raise the window shade and let in the afternoon light. Mory Masters groaned and turned on his side.

"Dad. Dad! Wake up for chrissake. Why aren't you at work?"

"Oh … Shit. Sorry, Bowie. Where is she? Nora … Bitch. Help me, Bowie."

"You puked on your shirt, Dad. Clean up. Go to bed. It's too late for work now."

When Morris Masters lost his job at UFC after two on-the-job accidents, unemployment checks, and handouts provided meager subsistence—enough for a time for the daily fifth of rot-gut and little else.

"I don't know what to do, Dad. Goddamnit, Dad, you useless piece of … Goddamnit."

# Chapter 3
# Bowie

By age 13, at six-foot one inch, Bowie Masters towered over most of his classmates. His size and reticence made him a constant target for toughs from the upper grades. He never lost a fight with them because he never fought except to cover himself from the blows that pounded him—the blows that relieved the real pain no one else knew about.

For the third time in a month, Bowie was summoned to the office of the Vice Principal. "Again, Bowie? I understand you have been brawling again. Want to tell me about it?"

Bowie had no words. He hurt inside and out. He was tired. He was hungry. He was frustrated. His bright, intuitive mind was no match for the "book learning" his school demanded. No one reached out to help his derelict father. No one sought to understand his pain.

Bowie Masters did not understand why society and his parents had failed him. Still, he knew with certainty they had and that he must now help himself outside of the system, without relying on support from anyone he had loved or trusted.

At last, he replied, "Guess I just fucked up again."

Bowie walked away from school. He took odd jobs with any tradesman who needed an extra pair of unskilled, low-paid hands, often working several at one time in an attempt to make ends meet. He learned skills quickly. By the time he was 16, his lanky body had acquired hard muscle from toting bricks and lumber and swinging a hammer or a mattock eight to ten hours a day.

His part-time bosses learned to rely on him and trust his work. One enquired, "What are your plans, Masters? I could use someone full-time."

"Damned if I know. Gotta take care of the old man. Know that."

Bowie Masters, with no vision of next year or even tomorrow, knew only today and payday. He paid the rent regularly. He fed and clothed himself. He bought his father's booze. Then, six years after his mother abandoned him, his father was gone too, along with the few dollars he had socked away in his bureau drawer.

*Good riddance, asshole. Except for my money. Sonofabitch!* And along with his righteous rage, the pain in his head grew more ferocious and frequent.

It was no problem for Bowie to forge his parent's signatures on the Marine Corps enlistment papers. He had done it for years at school. The school records were a bit more problematic, but $200 fixed that. And Bowie Masters had a new life, a new purpose, a new family— for a time.

Then, on an August morning during the eighth week of Marine boot camp, First Sergeant Edmond Bonners, fondly known as Little Caesar or Black Eddy, called Private Masters out of the ranks of hungry recruits standing in the pre-dawn grayness, ready to march to the mess hall for breakfast.

Masters' stomach growled as he reluctantly answered Bonners' summons. "Here, First Sergeant!"

"Report to the CO on the double."

Captain Bruce O'Brien, commanding officer of Wolf Training Company, was a career marine in his thirteenth year of service. He had joined the Corps after a brief career as a heavyweight boxer, from which he retired undefeated. As a young lieutenant, personal gallantry earned him a Silver Star and Purple Heart during the Persian Gulf War. Since then, his excellent combat skills and marginal proficiency ratings earned him only an assignment as commander of a recruit training company. Now, he simply hoped to retire undefeated from the Marine Corps—just seven more years of service.

"Private Masters reporting as ordered, sir!"

Captain O'Brien looked up from a thin file folder of paperwork to size up the husky young marine recruit who stood on the other side of his desk. He flipped a return salute. "At ease, Private."

Bowie Masters remained at stiff attention.

"Private Masters, I am sorry to say that, as of this moment, you are no longer a Marine." He watched Master's broad shoulders droop and dismay rise in his eyes. "You are guilty of falsifying statements on the Marine Corps Requirements questionnaires." He turned a page in the file on his desk.

"Number one: you are not yet 17 years of age. Number two: your high school diploma is a forgery. There is no proof you attended high school, much less graduated."

Masters stiffened again. "But ... but, sir. Permission to speak?"

"Never mind objecting, Masters. I can't help you. The orders are here. You're out."

"But, I'm a good Marine. Look at—"

The captain stood to interrupt the private.

"Listen to me, Private. You will receive a General Discharge, effective immediately. Pack up. You will be escorted from the base in exactly one hour." O'Brien closed the file. "You are dismissed."

"But it ain't fair. Sir. I ain't done nothin' wrong!"

Blind rage impelled him as he lunged at the captain across the desk.

Pain stunned him as a massive right jab broke two front teeth and dropped him in his tracks.

~~~

Three months short of his 17$^{th}$ birthday, Bowie Masters was without a home and without a job on the streets of San Diego. He had $300 of termination pay in his pocket, a set of Marine Corps utility fatigues on his back, and as much of his clothing issue as he could cram into a field pack. When he departed the recruit depot, no one had searched his pack at the gate. No one found the 9mm Beretta or 7-inch combat knife he had appropriated from the unattended quartermaster supply when he returned the rest of his government issue.

When he walked into the *Trux and Tourists* truck stop near the junction of interstates, he had a crushing headache, his jaw hurt, he was hungry, thirsty, tired and soaked in sweat. His sense of self was wounded even more. He loved being a Marine. Now, they too, had abandoned him. His clean-shaved head hung low.

The middle-aged waitress dropped her comb and mirror and left her stool behind the counter. "What'll it be, Sugar?"

"Double burger … no cheese … make it two. Large fries. And a super-size Coke."

The waitress managed a smile while she wrote wearily on her order pad. Bowie watched absently as she clipped his order behind others waiting for the single short-order cook. He continued to observe her while she tended the coffee maker and retreated back to the stool behind the counter to preen her hair and file her nails. *Something about her I don't like.* Something that reminded him of a painful past. He didn't need more crap today.

The AC drying the sweat on his back felt good. The food felt better. But the nagging headache and tooth ache kept him in a foul mood.

"Don't they feed you at that boot camp?" The tall trucker, seated two stools down, drained his coffee cup and laid some cash on the counter.

"Feed you a lot of Marine bullshit about honor and commitment and then kick your ass out on the street. Fuck the Corps, is what I say."

"Is that what happened to you? Or maybe I shouldn't ask."

Masters scowled in his direction. "Yeah. Corps ain't no different than the rest of them. Semper Fi, my ass. Ain't right."

He watched the trucker pull some bills from a fat roll secured by a rubber band.

"Lemme get your lunch, son. Would that be okay?" The trucker stuffed the roll back into his shirt pocket and stood to leave. "You need a lift anywhere, Marine? I need to be in Phoenix by nightfall."

## Chapter 4
## Big John

Walking toward the line of parked 18-wheelers, the acrid smell of exhaust from 20 idling diesel tractors hit Bowie Masters even before the deep rattle of their engines reached his ears.

The trucker at his side stuck out a ham and said, "They call me Big John. You have a handle?"

Bowie ignored the outstretched hand. "Yeah. Just call me Loser." *I wonder what this sonofabitch wants from me.*

Big John grunted and hit the remote to unlock both doors of the Kenworth Studio Sleeper cab.

"Okay then, climb in, Loser. You can stow your stuff back there."

Bowie hoisted himself up into the cab and heaved his field pack behind the seat. Looking back, he saw what amounted to a compact apartment—couch, television, microwave, fridge—even a small bathroom vanity with a water tap.

Big John took the driver's seat. "What do you think? Can't shower or shit, but otherwise a comfortable little home away from home, and I don't exactly have a home. Still, like to get back to Phoenix when I can. On the road every legal minute. Been coast to coast more times than I can remember. It's a lonely life, but I like it."

In the closed cab, Bowie quickly became aware that Big John's opportunities to bathe were indeed infrequent, while his acquaintance with deodorant was also limited. The pine-scented, hula dancer air freshener suspended overhead did little to mask Big John's emissions. The burly driver started the big rig, moving out while continuing a rambling series of personal revelations. He accelerated through a series of gear changes as they left the truck stop behind and rolled along on Interstate 8 East.

Miles down the highway, Bowie wondered, *Does this mother fucker ever shut up?*

As if to reply, Big John continued, "I'm leasing this tractor. Costs more for the extra comforts, but worth it. Take any hauling job I can find to earn enough to buy one."

*Like I care.* Bowie thought how nice it would be to grab a nap on the couch back there, to let the quiet darkness enfold him, to close out all this crap and maybe rid himself of the crushing headache that tightened its grip mile after mile, story after story.

The GPS warned, "Keep right on I-8 East."

During brief lulls in Big John's marathon memoir recital, the radio continued spreading the gospel in Spanish. Easy to tune out. Bowie knew only a few of the words and phrases though he'd been exposed to the language all his life.

Big John droned on. "Been on the road for six weeks this time. Phoenix is what I call home, though. Don't actually have a place there. Just a P.O. Box, and I do my banking ... stuff like that. Got a pretty little Mexicali Rose I stay with sometimes too, if she ain't busy with someone else. Sweet thing. Her name is Maria."

Bowie didn't bother to reply. He supposed he could call Phoenix home too, for now. Where else? Why not?

*Rock of Ages.* Finally, a song that Bowie recognized among the Latino hymns the radio station favored. It had been a favorite on the only station his mother listened to—a mélange of the Lord's platitudes and playlists. He closed his eyes. They were suddenly wet. Long time since he'd thought about that, about her.

Big John hummed along and sang an occasional word. At El Centro, Big John interrupted his thoughts again. "I'll be making a nice deposit after I drop this load. A few more, and I am ready to buy my own rig." He gave a short blast on the truck horn at a westbound Freightliner.

Bowie nodded, half asleep. "Hey John, mind if I use your apartment back there for a nap? I'm really drowsy, and those burgers ain't sittin' well, either."

"Help yourself, Loser. Toss your sack up here in the seat and climb on back. Stay hydrated, though. We still have five hours or more of hard, hot going ahead." As if to emphasize his words, the diesel engine coughed and the transmission complained as Big John geared down on a long upgrade. "Get a bottle of water from the fridge. This desert heat will dry you up like a prune. Hard on the truck, too."

Bowie shoved a pile of dirty laundry off the couch onto the floor. "Hey, Big John, what's this? Is it loaded?"

"No. No. Sorry. I forgot. Didn't quite finish cleaning my rifle. Just case it up and set it aside. I always keep it cased, unloaded and out of sight … real out of sight."

Bowie lifted the weapon and peered through the scope. Big John's ear loomed in the sight like a fat moth. "Pow. Pow."

The weapon felt good in his hands, better than the Marine carbines he'd trained with.

"Nice rifle. Do you hunt?"

"Yeah. Hardly ever have time … only small game. I really like it, though. It's a Winchester Model 70. Vintage, two-seventy caliber. Got it used. Still not cheap. Mostly use it for target shooting. Accurate as all hell."

Bowie cased the weapon and zipped the bag shut. He sat watching the scenery roll by. The 18-wheeler descended from the barren rocks of the high desert into the Creosote shrubs and cacti—the Prickly Pears, Organ Pipes, and giant Saguaros of the Sonoran Desert. He stretched out full length and closed his eyes.

Semi-conscious, Masters shivered, remembering the early morning cold again.

"Report to the CO … on the double."

"But sir …"

"… no longer a Marine!"

"What did I do wrong, Mama?"

Big John's voice intruded on his furtive dreams.

"Hey, Loser, did you ever see these sand dunes? We will be crossing from Colorado into Arizona in a few more miles. Yuma. You okay?"

"Fucking hot," Bowie mumbled and turned on his side.

Fitful visions incongruously superimposed with the music and the truckers droning voice.

"By the time I get to Phoenix, she'll be waiting...."

*Dad, Dad ....*

"Ama-zee-ing Grace, how swee-eat it is ...."

*It ain't fair ....*

"Hey, Loser. Here we are. Gila Bend. The armpit of Arizona. Shit, the armpit of the world. Heading north now."

The rig turned off the interstate onto highway 85. Bowie struggled into consciousness.

"Jesus, it's hot back here. Is the AC working? What time is it?"

"112 degrees at six en la tarde, courtesy of KCKY, AM, Mesa, the big voice of Jesus on your radio, 1150 on your dial. Fry an egg on the hood. Nothing to see. Get some more sleep is your best bet."

Sound, sweet sleep descended on him at last, and with sleep, the remnants of his rage and sorrow receded somewhere into cloistered memory.

Ninety minutes later, Big John pulled into a Loves station on the Papago Freeway, a place to spend the night before dropping his load in the morning. Not much going on this late. He called out, "Okay, Loser, this is it. You're on your own."

He glanced behind to where the young ex-marine still slept. "Wonder what you managed to make off with, courtesy of the U.S. Marines."

He retrieved Loser's field pack from the passenger seat and opened the buckles. Socks. Underwear. Fatigues. At the bottom, his hand found the Beretta and he removed it from the bag.

"Ah, well, look at this." He examined the weapon and checked the magazine. Not loaded.

Bowie awoke just then, shedding sleep in an instant. He looked around him, surprised by the lack of motion, quiet except for the throb of the idling diesel.

In spite of sleep, his head still hurt. He saw his open field pack and the Beretta in Big John's hand. "Sonofabitch!"

He sprang forward to wrest his belongings from the trucker, but Big John easily shoved him aside. "Not so fast, Sonny."

Bowie shoved his hand into the open field pack, found the combat knife and slipped it from the sheath. "I knew you would try to fuck me somehow, you Holy Roller sonofabitch!"

Big John dropped the automatic, drew back his arm and aimed a fist at his attacker. The seven-inch blade struck him under the armpit, slid between two ribs and punctured a lung. The second stab pierced a kidney, a third and a fourth time. Finally, Big John sagged, helpless, bleeding, and semiconscious.

Bowie watched the trucker's mouth gape open in shock, unable to scream, his eyes roll back, wide open. Still in a rage, Bowie plunged the knife into Big John's open right eye, then calmly retrieved his scattered belongings and stuffed them and the 9mm into his pack. Remembering the money, he reached into Big John's shirt pocket. He pulled out the fat wad and flipped through the bills. *Jesus, all hundreds but a few ... must be five or six grand here. Thanks, Bigmouth John.*

Bowie, at last felt good—no fear, no remorse, no regrets, the sudden violence a form of release. The tension was gone. His head was clear. He'd shown the mothers, the whole fucking bunch of them.

"I'll be leaving now, Johnny. Thanks for the ride."

He reached behind the seat to retrieve the Winchester, stepped down from the cab, and closed the door. "Have a nice day. I won't be seeing ya. Ya sure won't be seeing me."

## Chapter 5
## Billy the Kid

Wheels, a 1990 F150 Super cab. The purchase took most of Big John's money roll. In spite of a deteriorating paint job, an abstract blend of black and rust, the engine and transmission sounded good. Under 200,000 miles, if the odometer meant anything.

Bowie stowed his gear with the rifle Big John had contributed to his small arsenal behind the seat of the cab and pulled away from the Cruised-Not-Abused used car lot. With no plan and no destination in mind, he needed time to seek relief from the tension that nagged him, pulling the muscles of his neck and shoulders tight. He replayed the action of the past days for hours in his mind before he could focus on anything else. He felt no shame, had no regrets except that he'd left his good combat knife protruding from Big John's right eye socket. He liked that knife.

Hunger nagged him too, and he pulled into the first shopping center on the road. He ordered two Egg McMuffins and a large Coke at Mickie Dees and parked outside the Walmart Superstore. Finished quickly with his food, he locked the map compartment where the Berretta was stowed and made his way into the crowded store. First the Men's Room, then Sporting Goods and Men's Wear, then Groceries.

The usual long checkout line—only three out of thirty registers open. The kid in the cart in front of him yammered and slobbered, staring blankly at him and reaching out a small hand while her mother unloaded half the store onto the conveyer. Bowie stuck out his tongue. The kid followed suit and smiled, wide-eyed. Bowie showed her his middle finger. The kid giggled and returned the salute. Finally, Bowie stuck his thumbs in his ears and wiggled his fingers back and forth.

When the kid howled with delight, the mother turned, frowned, and hurried away with her child and cartful of purchases.

His turn, at last.

"Quite a load, Sir. Do you want me to pack most of your purchases into the storage bin and camping cooler?" The associate's name tag labeled her as Lucinda.

"Sure, Lucy. Great."

Everything fit except the one-man tent, the fishing rod and reel, and the baseball bat. He had new jeans, shirts and sweats, enough groceries and jugs of drinking water for several weeks if he was careful, and the inklings of a plan. Might be a good idea to stay out of sight for a time.

"Going camping? There are some nice spots in the park. Not too far."

Bowie counted out the cash payment. "Might do that. Don't know."

"Well, have a good day." Lucinda smiled warmly at her husky, young customer. "Thanks for shopping Walmart. Come back soon."

Outside, he hoisted everything into the bed of the pickup. He climbed into the cab, started the engine and the AC, and counted his cash. Seven hundred forty-nine dollars and fifty-five cents. He placed $700 in bills under the Berretta in the map compartment, along with the truck bill of sale and license application, and stuffed the rest of the cash in his shirt pocket.

He wondered if anyone had discovered Big John yet, *the thieving sonofabitch.*

The Coconino National Forest offered thousands of secluded camping spots and easy access to and from the interstate. In less than an hour, he turned off I-17. Pine branches scraped along the roof of the cab as he rumbled down unpaved roads and found a small clearing near the banks of a stream that branched into the Verde River a hundred yards downstream. No one else in sight.

The air was still warm at this elevation. The setting sun glinted off the water. Best get settled while there is light. The tent went up in minutes, following intuition rather than printed instructions, then peanut butter sandwiches for dinner tonight. He'd explore tomorrow. He crawled into the tent, zipped it shut, and was asleep as the moon rose through the tall pines.

In the morning, he washed in the stream. Returning to his campsite, distant voices startled him. He crept back downhill through a stand of aspen toward the river, using low shrubs for cover. Two canoes floated on the current. Then they were gone. He'd need to be careful.

Marine basic had not yet covered survival training when the Corps returned Bowie to the civilian world. He had learned to dig a slit trench to bury waste, and once, when he was eight, he had been sent to summer camp for a week. He could tie a few knots, paddle a canoe, recognize poison ivy, and tell a non-poisonous snake from a viper. But he knew the ways of the streets better than he knew the wilds.

He wondered how long he could subsist here, alone. Alone, except for whatever else might be living here. He had heard there were bobcats and bears, and he had seen a variety of spoor—droppings, hoof prints, and paw prints—near the stream, some kinds of critters, large and small. But he felt more at ease alone in the wilderness than he ever had at school, on any job, or even in the Corps. People? What good had people ever done for him?

*I will make it here on my own somehow. Fuck the rest of them.* After the second night in the forest, Big John's face no longer haunted his dreams, and the tension that tortured his head and strained his muscles abated.

On the sixth day of his wilderness odyssey, Bowie caught a fish, a big fish. Delighted with the thrill of newness and success, he laughed out loud. He'd never done that before, ever. For the past five days, he had lived on rice and eggs and peanut butter and jelly. But on the sixth day Bowie dined on fresh fish, sautéed in oil with potatoes and onion. Nothing had ever tasted this good. He doused the last coals of the campfire at dark and wondered if anyone might have seen the smoke.

He fell asleep nights listening to the low call of a Great Horned Owl and awoke most mornings to the chatter and chirps of finches, chickadees, nuthatches, and bluebirds. He knew these birds and others from the book he had picked up on a whim at Walmart—F*lora and Fauna of the West.* Real good book. Lots of pictures, not many words.

The deep hole just where the stream met the river yielded trout for more than a week, and on those days, trout was the dinner menu. Porcupine stew and barbequed jack rabbit were a nice, one-time diversion. The hunting knife from Walmart sporting goods was sturdy and well-honed, but he hated the skinning and gutting of small, furry game. Trout was his favorite. Then, with the waters running low after weeks without rain, fish of any kind became scarce.

He lifted the lid of the camp cooler to take inventory. Sixteen eggs, three wrinkled apples, five potatoes, one carrot, margarine, oil, half a pound of ground coffee, and three slices of stale bread. Besides a handful of assorted candy bars, that was the extent of his rations. *I'll have to move on soon, back into what the others call civilization. . . and what I call hell.*

In the fourth week of his hermitage, it rained—gently falling throughout the day. The dry earth revived, sending forth new growth and filling the air with the scent of evergreens. The steady rain became a drizzle. Reluctantly, Bowie began the process of packing up to leave the next day. It was almost dusk when he hoisted the storage bin, into the truck bed and unlocked the cab. Everything as he'd left it—cash, papers, weapons. He had time for one last look around before dark. Maybe his last night without human contact. Then he'd have supper and a good night's sleep.

Stellar Jays chattered above as he made his way to the stream. He hardly noticed that his jeans were soaked from the wet underbrush by the time he turned and headed toward the river. A red-tailed hawk swooped low and pulled a fish from the water. The fish struggled to escape the brutal talons as the bird rose gracefully into the air on widespread, strong wings. *Poor fucking fish. Good for you, big bird.*

Hummingbirds descended from the high branches of a Ponderosa to feed on the wildflowers on the river bank where Bowie stopped to stand among them. He raised his arms and eyes to the sky. The gentle rain washed his face. Tension drained from his mind and body, absorbed into the quiet beauty of nature. Suddenly, without warning, his eyes blurred with uncontrolled tears, and quiet sobs escaped from his lips. "Mama. Mama."

"Don't you know enough to get out of the rain?"

*Who's voice?*

He whirled to face the sound behind him. The voice was real. It fit its owner, frail and thin.

"Where the hell did you come from?"

"I'm camped on the other side of the rise. Saw your smoke a couple of nights. Decided to see who my neighbor is."

"Won't be your neighbor for long. I'm packing up and heading out tomorrow."

"That's a shame. Thought we might be able to team up a little. I ain't got much to share, though."

"I don't play on anybody's team but my own." Bowie took a closer look at the voice's owner. *Just a kid, even younger than me, looks like. Scrawny little shit. Skin on bones.*

"Got a name?"

"William. They call me Billy the Kid."

"Who's they?"

"Just folks I used to know. Been on my own for a year."

Bowie ran a hand over his head. The stubble of his military cut had grown out some. He wondered if he should let it grow to his shoulders like Billy's. Change of appearance might be a good thing. "You can share my last supper here if you want. Scrambled eggs tonight, 'bout all. Baby Ruth for dessert."

Billy the Kid's dirt-streaked face broke into a wide grin. "Real eggs? Great!"

"I'm Bowie," he offered hesitantly and stuck out a hand. The two boys shook and walked up the embankment together.

Sated and drowsy, Bowie and Billy sat gazing into the campfire. Bowie threw on some extra logs. Why not? No matter if someone sees it. He'd be gone at first light. "I have to piss, Billy, and maybe more. Mind the fire until I get back."

Three minutes later, the fire continued to burn brightly, but the fire watcher had disappeared.

"You have to go too?" Bowie called out. No response. He looked over to the tent. Then, the F-150 standing in the fringe of darkness.

The truck door stood open. Had he not locked it this afternoon?

He sprang forward. The storage bin stood safe in the bed of the truck. Then, the cabin.

The rifle remained where he kept it behind the seats. The glove box gaped open. Bowie reached in, desperately hoping against hope. The Beretta was gone. The $700 was gone.

"You little bastard. You won't get away with this." He slammed the cabin door shut and locked it. Too little, too late.

He snatched the Maglite and the bat from the tent and stood listening just beyond the light of the campfire. Hurried footsteps leading away toward the stream. Was it Billy Boy or some wild critter—coyote or bear?

There was a break in the clouds and a splash of moonlight as he advanced toward the sound of someone or something making its way through the forest. There and there—boot prints entering the stream. He shined the light upstream and downstream and across the water. Billy the Kid stood midstream, fumbling with the Beretta's safety.

Bowie charged. The Beretta flew into the dark water as the bat crushed Billy's right elbow. The boy screamed in pain. Bowie's voice became a growl. "Strike one." Billy the Kid howled and crouched, holding his arm. The bat split his skull back to front, and he fell, face first, into the stream. "Strike two!" Bowie said.

He sat Billy the Kid straight up in mid-stream and searched his pockets, rolling him gently from side to side. A few of the wet bills tore when he pulled them from a rear pants pocket. *Damn. Looks like the rest is all here, but the 9-millimeter is gone.* He dragged the body across the stream and under the shelter of overhanging branches, dropped it again face down.

"Strike three. You're out." Another betrayal. Rage against humanity again took possession of his soul, and blackness shrouded his mind.

## Chapter 6
## Selena, Isabella, and Polo

Many nights, he slept in the pickup. He called it the Ford Motel. On warm, clear nights, he lay sprawled in the open truck bed on his air mattress. On cooler nights, he made himself as comfortable as he could in the cab. Unclean gas station restrooms served as his personal care spas. At times he travelled by night and slept by day. At times he pitched his small camouflage tent in an obscure reach of a local park. His diet comprised a narrow spectrum of fast food—hotdogs, tacos, and on good days, chimichangas with rice or Big Macs and fries with occasional supplements of fresh fruit from roadside stands.

His immediate plan was to remain unnoticed, to keep moving, keep putting miles between himself and Billy the Kid's mangled body. *Shit, the scrawny little bastard deserved what he got.* No matter how far he travelled, images of the frail, frightened boy haunted his dreams and his waking hours. Tension gripped his shoulders and neck as he drove. Darkness shaded his vision as blinding headaches tortured him. Relying on large doses of Advil and Aleve for some relief, he drove the aging pickup, he pushed himself to move on, seeking only escape.

After weeks of aimless roaming, he camped on the outskirts of Yuma, just a few miles from what could be permanent safety. Two ports of entry to Mexico, Los Algodones and San Luis Rio Colorado, were within walking distance. But if he slipped across the border without a passport, he might never be able to return.

In October, harvesting of the citrus crop had already begun and would continue through the winter. He drove past groves of grapefruit, lemons, oranges and tangerines. Frequent postings on roadside signs attracted his attention. *He learned that Se Busca Ayudante or Se Necesitia Ayuda* were *Help Wanted* signs inviting migrant workers to harvest the orchards and fields.

He couldn't expect his money roll to last much longer, and a vagrancy charge could lead to worse things than hunger if the law started investigating. He found growers gave preference to hiring Americans over the 2A-H Mexican workers and illegals, who were much more knowledgeable and efficient at the harvest. The law required it.

Often, he was the lone American working the fruit groves or, when the vegetable harvest had begun in spring and summer, in fields of cabbage, cucumbers, lettuce, and peppers. He followed the mobile, temporary agrarian society as they followed the harvest but remained an unwelcome outcast. No problem, loner was his preference too.

He camped apart from his fellow workers in his tent and truck. The shabby temporary trailer housing they lived in was no attraction. He would have preferred the meals the women often prepared over open fires and in portable ovens to those provided by the employer or his own occasional meager efforts at cooking, but none was offered. Only the small children showed him any interest, in part because he gave them small gifts of candy he kept in his pockets for that purpose, in part because their parents warned them to stay away from the gringo.

He was alone, yet part of the swarm of workers that moved over the fields like a unified human machine. He toiled alongside his swarthy coworkers, putting in an honest day's work but unable to match their productivity. Oh well, the pay was the same. Whole families sometimes worked together—men, women, and children. Some adults carried their own machetes to harvest the cole-crops with expert swipes of the giant knife. Bowie rented his from the employer for a dollar a day deducted from his pay weekly. His cash reserve grew very slowly after spending $5 a day for meals. At least he didn't pay rent like the others crammed into the trailers.

Bowie was not entirely unnoticed. Selena, wife of the Mexican field boss, Polo, watched the young, muscled boy hunched over the endless rows, sometimes shirtless in the afternoon heat.

She nudged the other women working at her side. "Mira eso," look at that. "Si, mira, pero no toques!" they warned.

That evening, while her daughter, Isabella, was already asleep, she was determined to ignore the warnings of the women—look but don't touch.

Selena entered Bowie's tent. Clad in only undershorts, he lay groggy, on the edge of sleep. Alerted by her touch, he sat suddenly upright, reaching for the hunting knife he kept near at night. "Who the hell are you? What do you want?"

"Calla, chico, Soy Selena," she whispered. She stripped away her blouse quickly while he sat stunned but obediently quiet. She reached down. His involuntary reaction was strong and immediate. "Ah, pene grande." She bent willingly to the task. Moments later, he lay back, spent and smiling.

"Oh, muy rápido. Maybe you no make love long time," unaware she had taken his virginity into her mouth and was the first to share sex, such as it was, with the blithe, bewildered boy.

"Relajar." She pushed him back and lay beside him, massaging his torso with her hands and lips. His second erection arose quickly while she smothered him in her copious, matronly breasts and guided him with hip movements and squeezes. Later, she lay back smiling and satisfied for only a moment before dressing. "Adiós, Mi bonito." She hurried back before Polo finished his game of Mexican Poker and noticed her absence.

In the weeks following, Selena became a welcome visitor to Bowie's tent on all nights when cards or gossip or some other diversion kept the company of male workers safely occupied. The middle-aged matron taught the inexperienced young man nuances of sexual intercourse he would never have imagined and would never forget.

Isabella, now aware of her mother's absences, observed her visiting Bowie's tent. The teenage girl had also observed Bowie working alone in the fields, and her curiosity had grown with each passing day. The night following Selena's latest rendezvous, he received a surprise visitor. He needed no coaxing to respond to the wild, ardent kisses of the beautiful young girl. This time, he became the teacher and she the eager student. Afterward, he held her at his side while she wept silently in his arms.

Dawn broke, and Bowie dressed, ready to find an early breakfast and return to the harvest. Polo stood outside his tent, a machete pointing at his genitals. "Clear out, gringo! We don want you here!"

He considered his chance of survival if he ignored or opposed the irate Mexican labor boss. His bat and his knife were in the tent. His machete was in the truck. *Might not be fit for work or anything else even if I survived.* The vegetable harvest was almost finished. He would need to move on soon to find work elsewhere. Polo watched, glaring and muttering in Spanish, while Bowie loaded the tent and a few camping items into the F150 and drove off without stopping to inform the farm owners. *Damnit, just lost a week's pay. At least I gained a machete.*

"Hijo de puta!" Polo waved the machete overhead and watched the pickup slowly disappear from view. "Don come back! Sonofabitch." He spat in the dust.

Young workers' children along the road paused in their early morning game of soccer, waving and smiling. He would miss the children. He would miss Selena. He would miss Isabella. But it was time to move on, maybe risking more exposure. He would have to take the risk.

## Chapter 7
## The Double U

*What am I going to do now? I can't hide forever. I need cash to survive. I need to make a living somehow. That means people. The fewer the better.* He drove north and east, avoiding the interstates, avoiding Tucson and Phoenix. The cultivated fields gave way to a varied, arid landscape of forest and shrubs, cactus and grasslands, and into Arizona cattle country.

He drove under the high gateway arch of a ranch with the symbol of a capital U with the numeral 2 superimposed. *No idea what that means.* But the Help Wanted sign on the gate post was printed in English. He followed the unpaved road, driving past fields of grazing cattle and corrals of milling horses. He parked near a rambling, low-slung ranch house and approached the man on the porch under the wide-brimmed Stetson.

"Welcome to the Double-U family ranch. I'm Jasper Williams, owner. Looking for work?"

"Yeah, maybe."

"Can you ride?"

"Yeah ... sure." *If it helps get me a job for a while.* "You mean horses?"

"Yup. Can you cook, too?"

"Sure. Beans and stuff."

Jasper Williams cast a skeptical eye on the sturdy, tanned young man before him. "Well, I'm real shorthanded, and we're starting to drive the herd up north to the higher elevations. Not an easy ride. Think you're up to it."

"What's the pay?"

"It's $20 a day for however long it takes, maybe a few weeks, maybe more than a month. Payable at the end of the drive. Room and board included." He laughed. "That's a sleeping bag on the cold ground under the stars. Maybe a campfire if it ain't raining. And all you will care to eat. You might be cooking it."

"Okay, Mr. Williams. Deal." He wondered at his quick decision. This was a whole new world filled with strangers. Could he trust any of them? Still, it was obscurity, and he needed that.

"Got a name, sonny?"

"Bowie Masters."

Jasper stood and offered a handshake. "Then welcome, Mr. Masters. Head over to the bunkhouse and get acquainted with the two over there. I will see you at dinner. Probably don't have to tell you to come hungry."

Bowie was having second thoughts. "Anything you want to tell me about my job?"

"It will be just you three and me in the morning, four total. We need to move 1500 head of prime Angus to summer grazing—about 50 miles north. Being this shorthanded, it will take a number of trips, maybe 200 head each time. You'll be driving the wagon with the food and equipment most of the time. Ain't easy. Uncle Bob in the bunkhouse can fill you in some."

"What about Irv … that's my truck?"

"Might want to leave it under those shade trees. No one will mess with it while we're gone."

He moved the pickup, retrieved his backpack from behind the seat, hesitated, and stowed the rifle, machete, and stained baseball bat out of sight. He locked the doors carefully and patted the fender of his faithful friend. "See you later, Irv ... some time."

Eight bunks stacked two high lined the walls of the bunkhouse. A large wooden table with picnic-style benches dominated the center of the spacious room. Six rustic chairs were placed near windows in the unpainted walls that separated the bunks. Two more sat in the room's interior. A lanky cowhand sat in one, his boots propped up on the end of the table. He wore jeans and a faded, plaid flannel shirt. He glanced at Bowie and spit his chew into a tin can.

A gnarled, white-haired ranch hand also dressed in jeans and a torn plaid shirt sat on a bench at the large central table. He turned to watch Bowie enter the room. "Looks like the boss wrangled up a little help, Wes."

"Damn little, looks like to me, Bob." The voice matched the man's menacing exterior.

The white-haired man motioned to Bowie. "Come on in youngster. Toss yer stuff on one of the bunks. I'm Bob. They call me Uncle Bob 'cause I been here forever. That ugly hombre in the chair is Wes. He only graces us with his manly presence for the summer drive. Otherwise, he enjoys getting beat up by the rodeo bulls and broncs." He shook his head. "What d'you go by?"

"Bowie ... like the knife. Mr. Williams said I'd be riding out with you on the drive in the morning."

Uncle Bob eyed the new hand. "Had much experience with cattle drives, Bowie?"

Maybe it was time to confess. "Nope, none."

Wes snorted, "No shit, Sylvester."

Bowie said quickly, "But I learn fast, and I'll work my ass off."

Uncle Bob grimaced. "Let's hope that's enough." The dinner bell rang. "Let's go get some chow. Might be our last good meal in quite a few weeks. Wes, you gonna welcome our saddle mate?"

Wes stood. Six foot six inches of slim sinew and strength. "He stays outa my way, we'll get along fine."

Bowie trailed four feet behind the two men on the way to the ranch house. The air was cold.

The aromas of freshly cooked meat and vegetables greeted them inside. The Mexican cook delivered large steaming platters laden with roast beef, carrots, potatoes, and onions to those gathered at the polished wooden table that was set with real silverware, good China plates and large, clear glasses for milk or water. Plates piled with sourdough were already in place.

"Dig in. There's more where that came from. And apple pie for dessert." Jasper Williams introduced Bowie to the others already seated, some drinking wine or beer. Jasper's younger brother, Jack Williams, and older sister, Jennifer Williams, would remain behind to manage the ranch, along with the housekeeper, Ms. Smith, and the unnamed cook. Skeleton crew.

"Double-U has been a family ranch for more than a century. We still ranch the old-fashioned way with horses and wagons. Most cattle ranchers do, especially the smaller outfits. We like it that way. Seems like the cows like it better, too. The herd is all Angus now. Started out with Herefords, way back."

Jennie Williams inquired, "What have you been up to before you came to us, Bowie?"

He struggled to come up with something reassuring, something of value. "I've had some experience doing construction and farming and spent some time in the military. Haven't really been into ranching yet. Lookin' for something I might like to settle into."

"You seem so young for all that. You didn't care for the military?"

"Wasn't my thing, so I left after my three-year hitch. And I'm older than I look." He lied without effort, grateful that none of the men chose to dig deeper into his past but finished their meals in silence.

Jasper stood. "Won't be time for no more chit-chat. We need to sleep now and be ready to move out with the herd at dawn."

In early morning, over biscuits, bacon, and eggs, while Wes discussed the day's plans with Jasper Williams, Uncle Bob filled in a few details of the drive for Bowie. They would camp out the first night after covering about half the distance, sleeping six-hour shifts, two at a time. The waking two would monitor the resting herd on foot or by horseback. "Sleep with your boots on. If you hear a shout in the night, come running fast. Unless there's a problem, we'll deliver the cows to pasture on day two and all get a good night's sleep before we return to the ranch on day three."

Bowie asked, "What happens on day four?"

"Day four is the new day one. We start all over with the next batch. Now, finish your coffee, and I'll introduce you to the wagon team. We need to be ready to move out at dawn."

While Bowie watched, clueless, Uncle Bob demonstrated how to hitch the team to the equipment wagon—already loaded with rations for the trail—sleeping bags, clothing, shovels, picks, and sundry items that might be needed along the way. "I'll help get them out of harness tonight, too. After that, you're on your own." He handed Bowie the reins. "They don't understand much 'cept giddap and whoa. It's giddap you want now." And he walked away to mount his horse and join the drive.

The wagon team did not need directions from their inexperienced driver and might have even been unaware of him. They'd been over these trails many times. They knew the right pace. They knew when to stop and when to go. Occasionally, they needed extra urging on long uphill grades. Bowie shouted at them, handled the reins, and tried to appear competent. The ride was rough and grueling. He wondered if time on horseback might be easier.

Bowie knew eggs and bacon. Every morning, he scrambled a dozen eggs and fried them in the grease from the thick rashers. The small crew of four ate together as the sun rose. Roast beef or ham sandwiches fed them for lunch in the saddle, each rider stopping by the wagon individually. Jasper and Uncle Bob inquired how it was going or commented on the weather, always dry but colder at the higher elevations. If he spoke, Wes said only "What is it today, greenhorn?" He grabbed his sandwiches, filled his water canteen, and rode off. They consumed dinner hungry from a long day in the clean country air and with little grumbling about the menu, a huge pot of beans and molasses with fried ham or bacon, Texas slices of sourdough, and tin mugs of black coffee.

Before the start of the third drive after breakfast at the ranch house, Jasper approached Bowie, leading two saddled cow ponies. "Uncle Bob is getting a little saddle sore. Wants to know if you want to swap jobs for a while. He'll take the wagon. You ride with the herd."

Bowie had never been in the saddle. How hard could it be? He hesitated, scratched his head. "Okay, I'm in. I've watched how you manage the herd, but a little instruction on cow wrangling and herd riding would help."

He watched Jasper put his foot in the stirrup, reach for the pummel, and effortlessly swing into the saddle. "You want to get acquainted with your horse first off." He leaned forward, stroking the horse's neck. "Good horse." The horse nickered. "Now you mount up on Hank, and I'll watch. He's a good cow pony. Been on these trails many times and shouldn't give you any problem if you treat him right."

Standing on the ground next to Hank, Bowie suddenly realized it was a long way up to the saddle. He stuck his left foot in the stirrup and touched the horse's flank. Hank shivered and shied to the right while Bowie hopped on one foot to keep abreast. He grabbed for the pummel and heaved his right leg up with all his might. Made it. He searched for the other stirrup with his flailing right foot, almost losing his hard-fought mount on the nervous horse. Both feet secured, he leaned forward, stroking Hank's neck. "I'm Bowie," he whispered in the horse's ear, "guess we're in this together now." Hank did not reply.

"Now, pick up the reins. Hold them in one hand. Pull against his neck on the left if you want to turn right and vice versa. Not much else to it. Maybe a gentle kick with your heels on his flanks to speed up a little. Don't overdo it." Jasper demonstrated the moves, left then right, and trotted in a circle around Bowie and his patient horse. "Now you show me."

"Okay, Hank, move out." Hank did not move. "Let's go, Hank, forward." Hank did not move.

"Give him a little squeeze with your knees. Make a kissing sound if you know how."

Magically, Hank moved forward. "Good horse, Hank." Bowie did a left turn, then a right, then repeated the simple maneuvers. He relaxed a little began feeling comfortable in the saddle. The cow pony seemed to sense his ease and responded to his guidance without effort. He did a full circle, weaving left and right, finally returning, grinning and proud, to Jasper's side.

Jasper watched. "That will have to do. I will stay as close to you as I can on the trail behind the herd. Wes will lead. The cows that have made the trip before will follow him. The rest of them will trail along. We need to keep them bunched up as much as possible. You and I will zig-zag behind to keep any stragglers moving." He rode a little to the left and swung back to the right. "Uncle Bob will bring up the rear with the wagon and spare saddle horses, just as you did."

"Got it," Bowie exaggerated.

"Then let's get to work. Wes already has them moving out."

After twelve hours without his feet on the ground, Bowie ached from head to toe—and especially in between. The beans and bacon tasted great that night, and sleep descended without hesitation.

Before sunrise, Uncle Bob woke him. "Time to learn to saddle and cinch your pony. Let's go. Then we're on the trail again."

With the last of the herd moved to summer grazing land, the small posse of ad hoc cow wranglers gathered for one final breakfast together in the ranch house—scrambled eggs with lean pork sausage, stacks of flapjacks with syrup, warm biscuits with butter, mugs of fresh milk and Arizona oranges and grapefruit. And, of course, hot coffee.

Jack Williams handed the payroll money to his older brother, Jasper, who would remain at the ranch until time to retrieve the herd before winter. Jack would spend alternate weeks there or with Uncle Bob, minding the herd for the summer. Wes said he planned to join a rodeo as soon as he found one that would hire him. Might return for the winter drive. Might not.

Jasper handed Bowie $450 in cash. "You did fine for a greenhorn. Recon you earned this. There is a $30 bonus. You'll be welcome back any time." The two men shook hands. Wes nudged Jasper, who continued, "By the way, Wes says there's another fifty for you if you can drop him somewhere there's a rodeo with your truck."

He could use the money and had nowhere to go. "Okay, but let me check out the truck first on a little test drive. It hasn't been run for weeks." Wes and Jasper watched as he opened the hood, inspected the engine, and checked the oil. He replaced the dipstick. "It leaks a bit sometimes, but it's good now. Hasn't lost a drop sitting here." He mounted the cab. *Oh yeah, much better than a saddle.* He drove a short distance out of sight down the ranch road, stopped and hid the Winchester, machete, and stained bat under his camping gear in the truck bed, then covered it all with a small ground-cover tarp.

The two men stood waiting. "She's running fine. Hop in if you're ready. Let's go." It felt odd and satisfying giving directions to Wes, who climbed in without a word.

Conversation in the small space of the cab lagged, hanging unspoken like a dark rain cloud. Finally, Bowie asked Wes, "When do you think you might give up the rodeo circuit and come full-time to the Double-U?"

The question remained unanswered until Bowie thought it would remain so. Wes finally responded in his slow drawl, maybe Louisiana or Texas. "When I can't stay on the bulls eight seconds … or something gets busted up real bad. I know most of the rodeo managers, and they know me, so it ain't real hard getting signed on every year. 'Sides, Jasper can't pay what the rodeo does."

The prospect of some real income piqued Bowie's interest. Maybe to return the favor of transportation, Wes might answer his question. "Do you think I could work the rodeo, Wes?"

Wes pondered and chuckled. "Well, you learned to ride herd … and you didn't kill us with your cooking. Seems anything is possible." He let his words settle into the silence and added, "But damned unlikely if you really want to know."

He sat silent for a few minutes before he added, "Maybe as a rodeo clown. Real tough job, but pays more than the cowboys earn."

Bowie saw a glimmer of hope. "Mind if I tag along where you go, Wes? Would you put in a good word for me?"

"Sure thing. It'll only cost you fifty bucks."

## Chapter 8
## Lee Roy Johnson

By the time he teamed up with Lee Roy Johnson, Bowie Masters had gained 30 pounds, a Chevron mustache, three fractured bones, all the experience and wisdom acquired as a rodeo roustabout and rider, and a string of other odd jobs. His shoulder length hair was usually tied behind in a ponytail. At 27, a steely gaze had replaced the look of curiosity and wonder in his gray eyes.

He had returned to the Double-U after a few years on the rodeo circuit for one more drive while his broken ribs were healing. Sitting a trail horse was way more comfortable than a bronc or brahma. Jasper Williams greeted him warmly. "You're just in time for dinner. Be just us. The others are out for the evening" Over fried chicken and beer, the rancher and the rodeo rider caught up on new times and reminisced about the drive they once had shared. "Don't know what happened to Wes. Haven't seen him since that year you rode with us."

"We stuck together that first year when I left here. Should say I stuck with him on the circuit. Prescott, Peyson, Benson, Apache Junction. He cut out somewhere, and I lost track of him after that. How is Uncle Bob? He seemed kinda worn out that year I rode with you. Is he out with the others?"

"Oh, don't suppose you would have heard. Bob died the winter after that drive. Heart gave out. We called him Uncle, but he didn't have no kin. He's buried here at the Double-U where he spent so many years of his life. He did seem to have a fatherly interest in you, as I recall."

Three years as a rodeo clown and bull rider had punished Bowie's young body more than it had enhanced his financial status. Still, it was a living, something he could do, and the constant aches, breaks and bruises sometimes pushed aside the punishing headaches and the unbidden images of Big John and Billy the Kid that often invaded his mind. He wondered at times where his father had gone. Was he still alive? And what had become of Mama since she abandoned him all those years ago? That's when the darkest headaches tortured him, and he struggled to control hot tears that rose to his eyes.

Bowie moved from job to job, ever restless, ever fearful, ever on guard, never thinking of settling down somewhere. He'd been on the move most of his life. Several years he drove jeep tours around Sedona, Montezuma's Castle, and the Grand Canyon. That required memorizing a script describing eons of geological transformation and Native American ancient history, a task far more challenging than riding a bull. But something was lacking—the thrill, the sudden violence, even the pain.

Lone women tourists might be attracted to their young guide dressed in shorts and T-shirt. Stopping to chat at tours end and perhaps become better acquainted, they found him reticent and reluctant in attempted conversation. "Can you recommend a good restaurant for dinner?" might lead to them sharing a meal with him at an obscure but authentic Tex-Mex eatery. And after they picked up the tab, he might join them in their hotel room for a satisfying one-night stand. A few even tipped him for his services.

For the past two years he had entered the kickboxing ring, often against bigger, more experienced opponents. Quick, tough and agile, he learned to defend himself and how to disable an opponent without weapons, with just his hands and feet. He won the majority of his matches, not without paying a price. The illegals were the worst. Hondurans and Mexicans mostly. Used to tough times. Needy and greedy for the winner's purse. Tough and resilient, they wouldn't give up until a haymaker or a roundhouse kick laid them out. Neither did he.

"Quite a shiner you have there, young man. I wonder, sir, if you might tell me, how does the other guy look?"

Bowie looked up at the speaker sitting two barstools away: clean shaven, neat shirt and jeans, curly hair fringed with gray, broad, friendly smile, quite distinguished looking. He hesitated, always suspicious of the overtures of strangers. He had known black men before, of course. Young marine recruits from the city who spoke a language of their own and grizzled rodeo workers who rarely spoke at all, but none so neatly dressed or who spoke with such grace and eloquence as this dark stranger.

"Other guy used to be a bucking bull. They looked none the worse for wear. Now it's any broke roughneck trying to earn a few bucks or one of the paid performers who will get into the kick boxing ring with me. I manage to stay out of their way most of the time. But the crowd wants a bloody brawl, not cat and mouse."

"So, you say you were previously with the rodeo."

"Yeah, three years, but I had enough of that. Always somethin' in a splint or hurtin' or healin'. Didn't lumber, often suggesting some improvements. He drove sixteen-penny nails home with three blows of his hammer.

Lee Roy Johnson rarely contributed to the construction labor that he supervised. Within weeks, he recognized Bowie's abilities, raising his pay and delegating some of the supervisory chores to him in order to spend more time on procuring materials and the business end of building—payroll, clients, tax evasion. The Mexican crew learned to respect the man with the heavy hammer and looked to him to resolve problems daily on the job.

For the first time in his life, things seemed to be going his way. Yet the tension and headaches persisted. At their worst he yearned for the sudden violence of the rodeo or the kick-boxing ring to push them aside. That's when the nails submitted to his brutal hammer blows. Bam. Bam. Bam!

By the end of the year, Johnson had a proposal for his main man. "How about we partner up, Bowie? I'm slowing down. Don't seem to have the energy I should have to spend on the jobs, and you're handling much of it without my help already."

Watching Bowie's surprised reaction, he added, "I'll even give you top billing—Masters and Johnson. Funny, don't you think?"

Bowie missed the allusion to the sex scientists but smiled broadly. "Hell yes, Lee Roy. You're one of the few humans on the planet that ever treated me right. I'll be your partner, damned right." His guard was down. "I'll do anything you want."

For the next eighteen months, Bowie was on top of the world, building houses, building a life. Lee Roy Johnson became much more than a partner; he was a friend and mentor, maybe even the father he never had. At first, the older man invited the younger man to his home for dinner and talk. He learned that Bowie lived at the shabby Majestic Motel, at least when he didn't escape to his truck or tent for the pleasure of a night in the clean open, air. "I get a special price of $50 a week 'cause I'm steady. They make most of their income renting by the hour."

"Seems a shame," Lee Roy said. "I'm living alone in this big, four-bedroom house. It's the first one I ever built. A few minor errors, beginner mistakes I'd never make again, but first-class materials and construction. I have never wanted to put it on the market, even though it's a lot more room than I need with no wife or children to share it with. Move into one of the spare rooms and save fifty dollars a week."

Bowie hesitated to reply. Should he give up this much independence? Should he come to rely this much on another?

Lee Roy continued, "Board included. I have a first-class cook and housekeeper. Old Josephina ... been with me for years. I don't really remember how we met. She has a room too. Probably has nowhere else to go."

That day, Bowie moved into one of the spare bedrooms of the four-bedroom home on the outskirts of Mesa. This was pure luxury, but time spent with his benefactor was far more important. Lee Roy patiently tutored his partner in the business of home construction. Eventually he even came to understand the basic finances of loans and mortgages, supply and demand.

The two unlike men were together most of their time on and off the job, sharing the fine meals Josephina prepared, later relaxing from the day's labors watching television news of the war in Iraq, crime shows like CSI or Bowie's oddly favorite, Hell's Kitchen.

Sundays they rested, occasionally spending the afternoon target practicing with the Winchester rifle at a nearby deserted quarry. This was one place Lee Roy was the student and Bowie the instructor. He'd earned a Sharp Shooter medal in the marines. With the excellent precision of the Winchester, he was even more proficient. His shot grouping from 100 yards never exceeded a three-inch circle in the bullseye zone.

Bowie could not have imagined the feelings of happiness and comfort, of rightness with the world that had come to him by a chance meeting with a black stranger. If only he had met Lee Roy Johnson years ago, his life might have taken a completely different track. Now it almost seemed that Big John and Billy the Kid never happened. This was a new start, a new life, even purpose. Here was a friend who gave and never demanded giving in return.

Thus, Bowie gave the best he had to give, proud to share his achievements with his partner and friend, no longer fearful of his own psyche or abashed by rash unfortunate deeds of his past life. Not one for long range planning, he'd never considered where his own life might lead. Now he cautiously anticipated a bright future replacing a gloomy, desolate past.

Then Lee Roy Johnson died. Cancer, they said. And he was alone again.

# Chapter 9
# Morgan Morel

At 5:15 PM, the Director of Admissions and Recruitment tossed a file folder on Harlow's desk. "Glad you're still here, Harlow. The Dean must have someone on his ass. He passed this particular application to us for opinion and recommendations ... by tomorrow morning." He pointed at the large question mark scrawled on the front of the folder. "Check this one out carefully. He must have actually read it before kicking it down to us. Asked if this was usual. You will handle it, right?"

Harlow was the Associate Dean for Enrollment, a position with much responsibility and little power. His superiors often went to him for recommendations on any admissions applications that were not routine, the ones that took more than a little careful consideration to decide.

The Director offered, "Better read the applicant's required essay first. Get back to the dean with our decisions ASAP. I will back whatever you say." And he left.

Harlow grunted, "Thanks," opened the folder labeled Morel, and read.

<u>When My Parents Died</u>

Jules and Genevieve Morel, sped toward home on the rural Pennsylvania highway they had travelled many times before. Their 1997 Volvo sedan almost drove itself over the familiar stretch. Their young son, Morgan, was occupied in the back seat listening to Eminem on his new iPod while his parents joked, laughed and sang oldies in the front seat.

Late on that afternoon of June 30th 2003, the diesel engine of a tour bus coughed and sputtered to a stop along the shoulder of that same road. The driver, returning the empty bus to the shop for repair, had, as chance would have it, chosen the road less travelled by. He managed to pull the disabled vehicle almost completely onto the narrow shoulder in the shade of some roadside oak trees. He set a flare 30 yards behind it. He returned to the bus to call for and await help. None came. By early evening, he fell asleep.

The driver was jarred roughly awake at 8:38 PM when the Morel's Volvo struck the left rear end of the parked bus at full speed. The glancing collision sent the Volvo careening and tipping wildly out of control across the road, headlong into a line of dead tree stumps. The flare had died an hour earlier. It was the first death on the road that night.

I, unfettered by a seatbelt, was thrown free, ear buds still in place, dazed but uninjured but for a few bruises. Jules and Genevieve, my parents, died instantly.

At least, that has always been my hope.

They had been happy. We had been happy. No better parents have ever lived.

Ironically, because Dad was a shoe salesman, we lived on a shoe string, no savings or investments, no insurance, just able to pay the monthly bills on time. The legal and financial world would not notice their passing.

When they died, both at the young age of 46, they had no will. They had assets only sufficient to pay their few debts. But no worry—no relatives showed up to fight over what little they left behind.

When the shock of being alone left me, the realization of how we had lived came clear to me. I decided then to seek a career in law, specializing in financial and estate planning.

I want to—I must—dedicate my life and work to providing knowledge and legal tools to families in order that they may have a secure present and future for themselves and their progeny.

Thank you for considering my application to the Marquette University Law School and the Prelaw Scholar Program that can enable my dream.

Morgan Morel.

None of the usual self-aggrandizement and purposeful bragging. None of the customary citations of high school honors and accomplishments. But here was passion and purpose. Associate Dean Harlow reflected on how his own law career, his aspirations to represent the unfortunate, those least able to help themselves, had been cast aside for a life of paper shuffling at the university. Still, he could be of value to deserving law school candidates now and then.

Morgan Morel's transcript from the small high school in Door County, Wisconsin listed all "A"s except for one glaring exception, an "F" in Physiology and Hygiene in his senior year. A memo from the school principal confirmed that Morel had excelled in high school.

Entering our school in his junior year, Morgan adapted well. Although often reticent, he became well-liked by the student body and faculty. He participated as a member of the debate team and played second string guard on the basketball team. His academic record is the second best in the history of Gibraltar High School. His SAT score is 1700.

Harlow mused. *This kid has motivation and grades. No flaw so far. Wonder what he's really like.* He extracted a flash drive from an envelope attached to the file and plugged it into the USB port of the laptop on his desk. He clicked on the MP3 file labeled Morgan Morel.

The recorded phone interview included little more information but did address the single blemish on Morel's academic record.

"Hello, Morgan. I am calling from the Admissions Office of the Law School at Marquette University."

"Yeah, yeah. Hi. Hello."

"With your permission, I will record our conversation for future reference."

"Sure, sure. My pleasure."

The interviewer confirmed a few vital statistics, then asked, "Can you tell me about the one failing grade on your otherwise perfect record?"

"Oh, that 'F'? I got effed during that class alright. (Morgan laughs.) Actually, I never attended, but I did learn quite a bit about physiology in my own way."

The interviewer had not inquired further but recorded a voice note. "Morel offered no explanation why he never attended the class in Physiology and Hygiene."

What Morgan Morel left unsaid was that skipping that last hour class gave him and Nancy Feldstein 45 minutes to make out on some quiet byway in the Apache pickup before he pulled into the Feldstein driveway and dropped her off before continuing home from school.

Harlow stapled a page of his official stationery to the folder and wrote.

Definitely not usual.

I recommend admission of Morgan Morel to the Prelaw Scholar Program in the fall term along with a merit scholarship of ten thousand dollars ($10,000) for every year that the applicant remains enrolled. If we and he are worthy, he will receive a BS degree after completion of four years of study in the field of his choice. He will then receive a degree in Law with privilege of admission to the Wisconsin Bar after the required two additional years of specialized study in law and completion of all law degree requirements. I am confident that this young man will be an asset to the legal community in whatever capacity he may choose.

~~~

"Pitcher of Leinenkugel draft," Morgan shouted over the din of celebrating graduates after four years of the Marquette University Prelaw Scholar Program.

Angelica Giles sidled in next to him and planted a smooch on his cheek. "We made the first four years, Shrume, now come the last two ... the tough ones ... for our law degrees." She tugged his arm. "Come with me. We saved you a seat at the table."

Morgan grabbed the pitcher and followed. *Let's get this over with, so I can head north.*

care for invitations from certain cowboys to spend the night with them either. Can't say leaving was a good decision, even so, or that the ring is a better choice."

"I know what you mean," the stranger said. "I worked the rodeos many years back. Just a year was far too much for me. I'm a builder now. Johnson Construction. I'm Johnson. Lee Roy."

Bowie raised his glass of Sam Adams October Fest. "Name's Masters. Bowie Masters."

"Ever think of working construction, Mr. Masters? Pays better than the rodeo, and it is much easier on the bones ... unless you fall off a roof." He sipped his Irish whiskey "Might even earn double what the rodeo pays if you have any skills. I have a crew of four, and I'm looking for good help. We're fortunate enough to have more work than we can handle."

Lee Roy Johnson seemed straight enough. But so had all the others. Bowie finally replied, "I have some construction experience a while back." The thought triggered unwelcome memories of a decade ago, days of working to support himself and his father, the drunken idler. His father—and his mother—abandonment, the panic and pain. He set his unfinished beer on the bar and pushed the rush of feelings aside. He faced Johnson. "How much do you pay?"

There was no warm welcome from Johnson's crew of four Mexicans. They excelled at laying shingles and subflooring but had less talent for many of the other dimensions of house building that Bowie had learned as a boy. With Johnson supplying the tools he needed, Bowie quickly renewed the skills he had practiced as a young teen—framing, drywall, roofing, even running electrical wiring according to plan. He could read a whole house plan and make it take shape in concrete and

Angelica yelled to the gathered Pre-law graduates, "Hey, y'all, make room for Shrume." She glanced at Morgan an arm's length behind her. "I heard them call you Morgan Morel when they announced the honor students at the baccalaureate graduation. I never knew your real name. So where did Shrume come from?"

Devon Davis, a black mountain of a man with a soft voice and an easy smile, stood and threw a large arm around Morgan. "Guilty. I dubbed him Mushroom when we met. You know ... Morel ... mushroom? But you all nicked him even further, and he's been Shrume for the past four years."

A chorus of *Shrumes* and a round of hugs and handshakes greeted Morgan at the table. He was aware of his popularity and accepted it as given though he did not really understand it. Maybe it was the Paul Newman look, the baby blues, or the reluctant smile. Maybe it was that he listened more than he spoke. Maybe, for the less sensitive, it was just that he was generous with his money, always the first to buy a round, often bestowing thoughtful small gifts to college acquaintances for no apparent reason.

For many there, the steep cost of a law school education—some $60,000 per year—was a problem, leaving them to face years of debt after graduation. Not so for Morgan, or rather, for his dear uncle Emile.

## Chapter 10
## Uncle Emile

Jules Morel's older brother, Emile, and his wife of 35 years, Esther, had not been blessed with children, but Emile had been ordained with a keen business sense and a talent for accumulating money. He amassed a considerable fortune from years as an importer and merchant of exotic fabrics, selling his wares throughout the New England states. He had not seen Jules, 15 years his junior, since he'd struck out on his own forty years earlier.

On September 11$^{th}$ 2001, Emile, age 59, watched the destruction of the World Trade Center twin towers on television with the rest of a stunned nation. He decided then, after years on the road, to hang it up, retire, kick back, take it easy for once, maybe write a memoir. *You never know what's coming next.*

Searching for a quiet place to retire, Emile found thirty acres on the Wisconsin Door County Peninsula, partially wooded with a small lake, an old farmhouse and a barn. He and Esther flew to Green Bay, met the real estate agent and toured the property. Emile wrote a check for the full asking price that same day.

Esther loved the challenge of remodeling the old house, and by Christmas they had settled in to enjoy their quiet life on the idyllic rural homestead. She walked the mile-long trail around the lake every day, weather permitting. She joined a book discussion club in Fish Creek and took up painting seriously again. Together with Emile, she frequented the shops, galleries and restaurants in the quaint hamlets of the scenic peninsula known as Wisconsin's Cape Cod.

With enticing new scenes to paint, Esther's artistic talent began to flourish again, while Emile chafed and itched for more purpose to his days than fishing for walleye and perch, tending his small vegetable garden, and following his dear wife to one or another of the many art shops that populated the area.

He wondered what had become of the family he'd abandoned years ago. He searched Yahoo and Google for the Morel name. He discovered hundreds of mushroom recipes. Finally finding a J. Morel in Pennsylvania, he mailed an inquiry to that address. Yes, this was Jules Morel, and yes, he had once had a brother Emile but had lost all contact years ago. That Christmas, Emile happily mailed out his one and only greeting card to his younger brother, expressing joy at his discovery and a desire to effect a personal reunion. His card and letter were never answered.

Then one day Morgan Morel called. "I guess you don't know who I am. We've never met. I found your number on a Christmas card you sent Mom and Dad last year. Jules and Genevieve? I am their son. My name is Morgan." He went on to describe the accident that killed both of his parents. "I've dropped out of school. I don't really know what to do now." He explained that he was alone and quite uncertain how to handle the estate—the few assets, the many small debts, the legal issues. He didn't ask for help.

"We will be there tomorrow," Emile offered immediately, "is the address still correct?"

Five weeks later, the house in Pennsylvania, the furnishings and few other belongings of Jules and Genevieve Morel were sold, and the debts were settled.

Esther held Morgan's two hands in her own. "I am flying home tomorrow, Morgan. We both want you to come live with us, just like we talked about yesterday and days before. Please say you will come with me."

Alone and underage, Morgan had no better choices, no future plans. "I'll pack up what's left of the stuff in Dad's old pickup and drive out. Uncle Emile should go with you now. I'll be there in less than a week."

"Promise? You're so young to make such a trip alone."

"I Promise. I'll be fine." But his confidence did not match his brave words.

Morgan loaded three suitcases of his clothes and two Rubbermaid storage bins of his personal belongings—books, DVDs, CDs, a PlayStation 2 and his Apple MacBook—into the back of the '59 Chevy Apache. He stared at the vacant house for long minutes, the home of his childhood memories. There had been no goodbyes when his parents died. There was no one now to say goodbye to. A new family would move into the cherished homestead tomorrow, displacing the ghosts of yesterday.

He climbed into the cab of the pickup, cranked the old engine into life, and started the long drive west.

Taking the roads less travelled, the Apache was steady but not fast—just what Morgan needed now. At times, with music in his earbuds recalling better times, he might laugh aloud. At times, with a sudden flood of tears blinding his vision, he slowed the old pickup to a crawl. At times, he sat still and alone with the engine rumbling on the shoulder of a roadway that somehow evoked a bright or tarnished memory.

He camped out on his way through Ohio, Indiana and Illinois, along the country roads, in small county parks or in a quiet corner of a gas station or grocery in some town without a name. His self-confidence grew with every mile and with each new town. A clarity and a new surge of interest in life began gradually displacing the clouds of grief and depression he had lived under since his parents died.

In Wisconsin, he drove north but remained three days within easy reach of his aunt and uncle's home, still reluctant to leave the past behind, unready to fully embrace a new life in a new location with people who were strangers just weeks ago.

Finally, on a rainy evening in late August, he pulled into the entrance to the long and winding drive to the rural homestead, turned off the truck lights and slept through the night.

At dawn, Morgan cranked down the window, stretched and yawned. The morning air was sweet and cool. The Apache awoke too as he turned the ignition key. He proceeded forward and rumbled to a stop facing the old, two-story farm house that was to become his new home. He stepped out of the cab and waited as the sun rose over the trees.

"Morgan. Morgan. There you are at last. You had us so worried." His aunt ran from the porch to greet him. "We expected you days ago. We were about to call the State Patrol."

Aunt Esther held him at arm's length while she delivered her mild admonishment, then she pulled him into her welcoming arms.

Whatever qualms Morgan had about this move and his newfound family were quickly dissipated by the natural affection his aunt and uncle held for him in the weeks and months that followed. It was as if Morgan was their own true son, the son they never had, an undeserved late blessing to their lives. He, in turn, guardedly and hesitantly, fell in love with them. His guilt for the receding memories of his parents diminished. They would never be far away in his memory, much less ever forgotten, but his life shifted from neutral into low. Morgan Morel, at age 17, was ready to move forward again, though his direction remained uncertain.

The essay he submitted with his law school application two years after resuming his life with his aunt and uncle described, part truth and part fiction, his motivations to study law. It was Uncle Emile who had encouraged him to apply for law school when he displayed no apparent direction or interest other than Nancy Feldstein for months following high school graduation.

Esther had pleaded, "Emile, you must speak with Morgan. Since graduation, all he does is work on that truck and visit that girl. He sees you puttering away your time and thinks he should do the same. Talk to him. Please."

At dinner, Emile broached the subject. "We've been wondering where you want to go to college, Morgan."

"Well ... haven't thought much about it."

"I can afford to send you to any school you choose, but you must choose."

"Why don't you teach me the trade?"

"You don't want to be a peddler like me. You're a smart kid. Get your ass in gear. Become a professional. I would have been a lawyer if I'd had the chance. Didn't have two dimes to rub together then."

 Morgan thought over his uncle's suggestion and decided, *Yeah, the law. Maybe that is really what I want to do. Need to do.* He recalled his parents' lack of ability to make good financial decisions. He remembered his own confusion and desperation when they died. He researched law schools, discussed them with his uncle and sent his application off to Marquette University in Milwaukee the next day. Indecision was not one of his shortcomings, and contrivances—the ability to spin the truth to his own advantage—had always come easily to him. Excellent qualifications for a career as a lawyer. He could, as the old cliché asserted, sell refrigerators to Eskimos in January. He did not talk much, but when he did, people listened.

 Now, four years later at the pre-law graduation celebration, Morgan took a few swigs of beer but declined the invitation to sit with his friends at the table. "Sorry gang, I have to drive home. Aunt Esther called. Uncle Emile is acting strange, not like himself. She is worried as hell. She needs me." He planted a smooch on Angelica's forehead and left.

## Chapter 11
## Esther Morel

Esther Morel, at age 65, loved two men. She was the faithful but troubled wife of one of them. The other, who had captured her heart and fulfilled her life after almost four decades of marriage, was less than half her age.

Esther hummed a broken melody working in the kitchen—she loved the kitchen of the old farmhouse and her place in it. It was where you might find her at any hour of the day, a sort of sanctuary with wide plank floors, a high ceiling, and the wonderful aromas of fresh baked bread and pastries. It was the heart of her home with Emile on its small acreage away from the neighbors but still close to surrounding towns.

She bent to kiss Morgan's cheek while she picked up his breakfast dishes. "Good boy, you cleaned your plate," she teased. But she was pleased he had clearly enjoyed the simple meal—three farm-fresh eggs, thick rashers of bacon, warm biscuits, and butter. "Are you ready for strudel, now? I baked it this morning. Still warm."

"I can't, Mama. Thanks. Breakfast was great, and I am stuffed."

Esther loved it that he called her Mama. He had started that only weeks after he had come to live with them. Was it five years ago already? It made her feel special. Their unofficially adopted son still called her husband Uncle, though she knew he loved him too.

She brought mugs of fresh coffee for the two of them and sat across the country trestle table from the object of her affection. "Did you like the eggs? My Araucanas are producing now. Enough that I can take two or three dozen to the market in town every week. I get a premium. The town folks go for the green shells and the dark orange yolks. The little extra cash comes in handy. Emile has gotten so tight with the money lately, and most of my savings went to fix this old place up. I can't even afford new art supplies now."

"The chickens must be happy with their new coop and run Uncle Emile and I built for them when I was here on Christmas break. I'm sorry I wasn't able to visit again until now. Senior year was so busy."

She had missed the boy, the young man, every day for the past four years when he had been away at school. It hurt her that he had not visited during the recent semester break, but she would not think of hurting him by saying so. Was he spending time with a new girlfriend he wasn't telling them about? Was there some problem at the university?

She said, "Do you like the new kitchen furniture? Remember, we ate at a card table before. It is all Amish. Old and new. I got the table out of a barn way over by Trempealeau. Red Oak. Chairs don't match, of course. We found some stuff at … uh, let me think … Cashton. Those ladder backs outside of Lacrosse. Other places."

"Really beautiful, Mama."

Esther's voice trailed to a whisper. "I loved those furniture-hunting trips with Emile. Reminded me of …." She paused for a long while before continuing, "Emile fixed them up. New glue and such. I refinished them." Esther smiled proudly. "And it's all way better and less expensive than new."

"That's great, Mama. Doesn't Uncle Emile eat breakfast? He was always an early riser."

"I don't know what to expect anymore." Esther turned away to hide her face. "He's changed, Morgan. Lost interest in things. Sleeps late. Roams the house at night. I found him in the barn one morning. Now I lock the doors. Of course, that upsets him too. And he swears at me sometimes! I could cry."

"Is he depressed or something? Maybe it will pass."

"He can't tell me what's bothering him." A low moan escaped from deep within her. "He is so angry sometimes and confused. It frightens me."

Morgan rose and stood behind her, holding her thin shoulders while she shook with quiet sobs. "I'll try to talk with him today. I'll see if he wants to go to town or maybe fishing. He likes to talk a lot then."

She sniffled. "He's so proud of you, Morgan. He can't wait until you get your law degree."

"Just two years more and I'm done. Piece of cake. I love you, Mama."

"Love you too." She wiped her eyes on a napkin. "I hear him upstairs now."

~~~

Emile Morel willingly accepted Morgan's invitation to drive into town, a chance to get away, to escape what must have begun to feel like incarceration, trapped by the walls of the old house and by forces he did not understand.

When they arrived at mid-morning, the breakfast crowd had already dispersed from Land-O-Cakes, Emile's favorite eatery. "Best Swedish pancakes and crepes in Wisconsin!" Emile used the last scrap of pancake to wipe a dab of Lingonberry jam from his plate. "You should try them, Morgan."

"I'm good with coffee, Uncle. Aunt Esther fed me at the house this morning. Do you want seconds?"

"To tell the truth, I could eat more. But Esther will be upset if I don't eat the lunch she fixes for me every day. And we must be home at noon."

"Ma ... uh, Aunt Esther is a little worried about you. Are you feeling okay these days?"

"Ah, Esther. She worries too much."

"She loves you, Uncle, so she worries." Morgan drained the last of the cold coffee from his mug. "She says you are a little rough on her sometimes."

"Rough? Rough!" Emile frowned.

"Says you swear at her and get angry. It frightens her."

"My god! That woman knows I could never harm her."

The young man and the old man remained silent, watching the sparse traffic passing the café window. "Can I bring you anything else?" The waitress interrupted their silence.

"Nothing for me, thanks. Uncle Emile?"

But Emile had left the booth, left the café, left the young man he thought of as his son. Now, he sat at the counter of a different café at a time earlier in his life when another waitress had asked, "Can I bring you anything else?"

Her name was Esther, he had learned as they chatted easily and that she lived alone, was his same age, graduated high school cum laude, and loved movies. "I'm alone here tonight. Would you like to go to the movies with me? Easy Rider is playing just down the street."

Emile loved everything about her—the touch of her hand, the scent of her close to him, the sound of her laughter. But the hand on his shoulder now and the voice calling his name were not Esther's. "Uncle! Uncle Emile. We should go now."

~~~

Esther picked up the stranger's dinner plate and asked, "Will you want dessert or coffee?" She had to admit she had an attraction to the young man. He was quiet and polite. Said please when he ordered and "yes, please" or "no, ma'am" when she asked if he needed anything else. And he was good looking—*cute* she thought. He said his name was Emile, just passing through.

She agreed to go with him, although she had seen the movie twice before. "You'll have to wait until my shift is up, though."

The stranger reminded her of Peter Fonda—but with shorter hair. She did not resist when he draped an arm around her shoulders during the picnic scene. And she yielded to his long, soft kiss when he left her again at the diner two hours later.

"I will be back in three weeks," Emile said. "May I see you then again?"

Her heart pounded until she thought he would hear it. "You can come to the diner."

Esther and Emile were wed by a Justice of the Peace in Scranton, Pennsylvania, one month to the day after they met. The honeymoon, one night in Motel

Scranton after a celebration dinner at *Jake's Steaks*, was almost as brief as the wedding ceremony. Emile had to be in New York City on Monday morning to receive a shipment of goods. "You must ride along with me, Esther."

She was thrilled to do so. She had never been to the city before. She had rarely been more than fifty miles from home. And she could not bear to be away from her new, beautiful husband.

They roamed the Northeast together, living in cheap motels, Emile peddling his wares, she at his side. "We are vagabonds, Emile. Free as gypsies. I did not know life could be like this."

"Someday, we can do it on a Harley, with the wind in our faces. Really free."

Weekends when they did not have to travel, they stayed in bed, made love, and ate pizza or Chinese while the television cast moving shadows across the room. Sometimes, they went to the movies. Sometimes, Esther wondered what the future would bring.

"What do you think of having children, Emile?"

"Where would we put them, sweetheart?" he answered with a question.

Another time, she implored, "You need to take some time off, Emile. R and R. You work all the time while I play or do nothing. It does get boring for me while you are busy."

"Sure. I will. Really. But first, we need to be in Newark all next week."

Driving through the Green Mountain Forest in autumn, Esther said, "Emile, you are somebody. You have a business. You know many people. You earn a lot of money."

She knew she should not resent her husband for these things. After all, he was honest and hardworking and provided for them both, including her generous allowance. And he asked nothing from her but her love and support.

"But I am nothing."

"You are my wife."

"That is not enough, Emile."

"I thought you liked our life together. Free ... on the road."

"I do. I did. But I need more. I need to do something, to be something ... somebody."

"I don't know ... what do you want me to do?"

The following spring, at Esther's suggestion, the inseparable couple rented a small apartment in New Haven. It was a central location for Emile's major suppliers in New York City and Boston. And it was convenient for his business trips, allowing him to return home to spend the night with Esther on occasion. Other times he might be away days or even weeks before the two reunited. He continued his travels, building his clientele, always larger, always more demanding.

Esther remained alone in the apartment, occupying herself with keeping the books for Emile's business and confirming appointments for his next road trip, missing their togetherness.

"I miss you, sweetheart." Esther almost sang, elated at the sound of Emiles's voice on the telephone.

"I miss you too, darling. How is this trip going?"

"Great. People are buying. But without you ...."

Esther cried herself to sleep that night. *This is not the life I hoped for.* In the morning, she went walking without destination, hoping for inspiration to restore joy to her life and marriage. She wandered onto the Yale University campus, watching students dashing between buildings or idling in groups, laughing and smiling. *What a wonderful life this must be.*

She happened upon the University Art Gallery and timidly entered its wide doors. Room after room of fine art, ancient and modern. Degas, Van Gogh, Picasso. Ancient sculptures, Tang-dynasty artwork vessels. A world of beauty beyond imagination. She was about to enter the sculpture garden when a guard warned her, "Closing in five minutes, Miss."

Where had the day gone? She returned day after day. She learned the university's fine arts program was among the best in the world. She visited the university library, spending days simply browsing the collection or researching art and artists. Off campus, she discovered small art galleries with exhibits of local artists and students. At one, she read a small note posted with others on a board near the exit. *Individual art lessons. All media. All levels of experience.*

The next day she used most of Emile's allowance to reserve her first week of instruction, purchase brushes and pencils and paints and canvases and notebooks. She felt alive again.

By the time Emile retired 30 years later, Esther was somebody too. Her acrylics and watercolors were in demand in small galleries and gift shops throughout the Atlantic coast. Several times, she had joined Emile on the road once again at his request. She enjoyed it, recalling their early days together, though it lacked the charm it once had held for her. Most of the time, she was far too busy painting or attending some civic organization meeting as a member or invited speaker. But always, when Emile was at home for a day or two, all that was put aside.

Then, in 2001, Emile retired unexpectedly. For the first time in their long marriage, they would have a real home, a house, and a garden, the American Dream.

And the second love of her life called one day. "Hello … my name is Morgan."

## Chapter 12
## Hermit

Books, luggage, and his few personal paraphernalia were loaded into the aged Apache before dawn. Morgan chose US 41 to head north out of the city. The tension and stress of the past months and years eased as the streets of Milwaukee gave way to open fields, already green with crops or spotted with herds of dairy cows grazing in the early morning sun. Tall silos stood guard over red barns and white farm houses. The sparse highway traffic thickened as he passed the outskirts of the larger towns and cities on his route—Fond du Lac, Oshkosh, Green Bay. He continued north on state road 57 until the familiar county roads greeted him for the last stretch home at last. *This is good,* he thought. *I should not have neglected Mama and Uncle Emile these past few years, but ....*

The final two years of the Marquette law school program had challenged Morgan Morel far more than any previous experience. High school had been a breeze, the first four years at Marquette more demanding. But for the last two years, study hours were unrelenting; his burgeoned brain was crammed to capacity with details of civil procedure, contracts, legal methods, property law, and torts. Study consumed him, yet he spent extra, unnecessary hours reading fascinating accounts of criminal cases at the Eckstein Library. Friends faded away. Those few who remained dubbed him Hermit. *Better than Schrume,* he thought. But time off for a trip home to visit his beloved aunt and uncle had been simply impossible.

With fall semester exams over in December, Morgan finally read his aunt's note, carefully scripted handwriting with her Christmas card.

*We miss you, Morgan. Study comes first. We know that. I pray every day for your hard-earned success. Soon you will have your law degree and be admitted to the bar. Emile will be so proud. Maybe that will help him be his old self again. We love you. Merry Christmas.*

He closed the card with mixed emotions of shame and love. The note was signed, *Mama*.

Then, he had heard nothing more until the phone call a week before graduation.

"I'm sorry, Morgan, we cannot attend your graduation."

"Oh, Mama, is there a problem? Did Uncle—"

"I can't travel with Emile, Morgan, and I can't leave the poor man alone."

He felt a sharp jab of conscience when she continued.

"He forgets things. He's confused. I must help him shower and care for himself. But I won't bother you any more with our problems. Are you okay?"

"I'm fine, Mama. Just so damned busy these last few weeks."

"Don't swear, Morgan, it's not professional."

"Okay, Mama, sorry. I guarantee I'll pack up right after graduation and come to see you, but I can't come right now. Maybe Uncle Emile's problems will pass."

He thought he might have heard a gentle moan before the phone went dead without goodbyes.

Only Angelica Giles helped him celebrate on the day they both received their law degrees.

"What now, Hermit?"

"No definite plans yet."

"Have you interviewed anywhere?"

"Thinking of going it alone." He watched Angelica's eyes widen. "Set up a small office back at home."

She smiled. "You'll starve."

He winced. "Well, people up there can use some good legal advice. Maybe I'll do some financial consulting too. I don't know. I've been reading a little about criminal law and criminal behavior in the library. Really interesting. Just a hobby. Can't think how to earn a living with it."

Morgan knew it was his turn to inquire about her plans. He knew she would be reluctant to part, probably to lose touch forever. He thought of the time months ago when they had slept together just once. For him, at least, it was diversion from the steady tension of the books, the pressure to succeed. "You?" he finally managed to ask.

"I can step into the family firm in Chicago if I want."

"Do you want?"

"Maybe."

Angelica raised her eyes to Morgan's, tears brimming. "I have a gift for you, Hermit." She pushed a small rectangular package over to him.

He smiled, a rare gratuity for her, and quickly unwrapped the gift. "I can't accept this, Ang. I didn't get anything for you. And it's way too expensive."

"It's an iPhone. The latest."

"I know."

"It's so you can remember me and maybe call sometime."

"I really can't, Angie."

"Damn it, Morgan, take it, for my sake."

They sat quietly in the nearly deserted coffee shop, glancing at the wall and empty chairs, he avoiding eye contact. She rose at last to stand at his side. She gently kissed his cheek. He studied his latte cup.

"Have a good life, Morgan. Maybe call me sometime. And get a haircut."

And the hermit was alone.

~~~

He pulled the Apache into a Mobile station, filled the tank with regular and grabbed a coffee and two filled donuts for himself inside the convenience store. *I'd best call them to let them know I'm on my way.*

"Should be there in an hour or so," he informed his Aunt Esther.

"We're so excited, Morgan. Emile can't wait to see you. He has a grand surprise for you. Our graduation gift." His aunt's voice was cheerful again. "He's been full of energy since I told him you are a lawyer now …

and coming home at last. I'll have lunch ready when you get here. Is there something you would especially like?"

"Just seeing you and Uncle Emile is all I want, Mama."

The old couple's surprise stood between the house and garage, glinting in the noon sunshine. A little slumped but beaming, Emile stood beside it. He'd been waiting there since just after sunrise. Esther watched from the wide front porch as Morgan embraced the gray old man and turned to survey his $20,000 surprise, a shiny new Harley.

"It's for you," the uncle said, "I always wanted to ride, but now I can't. You ride for me."

It was the perfect gift. Carefree rides on familiar lanes and roads, the wind riling his shaggy hair, shed all the stress and worries of the past months. Morgan quickly adapted from pickup truck to motorcycle, learning all the nuanced handling of the Harley, a Softail Slim, first short rides close to home, later all up and down the Door County Peninsula. On impulse one day, he turned into the Feldstein farm drive, eager to show off his prize bike.

"I hear that you're a lawyer now."

"Yes, sir." He still felt somewhat intimidated by the girl's father. "How is Nancy?"

"Lives in Green Bay now. Married. Two kids. Visits here with them now and then."

Morgan felt a catch in his throat, remembering. "Please give her my regards."

"Will do."

The Harley threw gravel across the lawn as he spun around and headed home.

~~~

"I love the bike. I love riding," Morgan informed his uncle and aunt. "If you will allow me, I want to take a long ride, probably explore some western roads. I know you haven't seen much of me, but I haven't had a vacation in six years. Since my trip from Pennsylvania, I haven't been out of Wisconsin."

"No, no Morgan. Don't feel bad for us. The bike is for you to ride. But you must get a helmet now or we will worry too much." His uncle shook a finger in his direction, and his aunt nodded her head in vigorous agreement.

He felt a tinge of shame. He knew his uncle would be a vicarious passenger on the bike while his aunt worried and missed him. But, one week later his plan was complete. He would head west into regions he'd never explored, following impulse and intuition. He packed a small duffle with clothing, rain gear, camping equipment and essentials. He bungeed it and the one-man pup tent he'd bought at Walmart behind the seat of the bike, to be ready to go in the morning, eager to begin a month-long adventure free of study and responsibility.

Morgan awoke early, though he had not slept much, anticipating the days and weeks ahead. He expected to ride at least 1000 miles and would take them slowly, absorbing the ambiance of each new mile as the roads rose up before the bike. His mind would be clear of textbook exams and concerns of a future life. The ride would be his only occupation.

There would be stretches of traffic on interstates, a driving experience he had yet to learn, and there would be quiet jaunts on scenic country roads. No timetable, no schedule, no agenda, as ad hoc now as the past six years had been structured.

Esther and Emile waited in the kitchen as he bounded downstairs from his bedroom. She had breakfast already on the table, a full course meal with fruit, ham, eggs, waffles, muffins, milk, and coffee.

"I'm sorry, Mama. I'm too excited to eat, and I want to be on my way." He downed a muffin quickly, hardly savoring its flavor, and sipped the mug of fresh, hot coffee, hoping to appease what he knew would be her disappointment.

As he finished, Aunt Esther handed him a cloth sack. "Some snacks for along the road."

The sack was full and heavy. "Thanks, Mama, you didn't have to do that." He stepped toward the door.

"Wait," his uncle interrupted him, "Take this too. You might need it. I always carried it when I was on the road, alone or with Esther."

Morgan examined the pearl-handled .32 automatic his uncle placed in his hand. "I appreciate it, Uncle Emile, but I'd rather not take it. I don't think I'll need it. We best give it to Mama and keep it here at home to protect the two of you." He saw disappointment in his uncle's eyes as he hugged him. He handed the pistol to his aunt while she enfolded him in her strong arms.

Then, he said his I-love-yous and was off on his road adventure.

# Chapter 13
# Son of Satan

The sun had burned off most of the early morning fog. It still hugged a few low-lying dips in the narrow, shaded county roads. No hurry. Then the bike sped southwest out of Green Bay, and Morgan followed a familiar route near the shores of Lake Winnebago. As morning commute traffic started filling the lanes, he abandoned the route, taking Wisconsin 23 west from Oshkosh. His spirit lifted, his pulse slowed, traversing rolling hills and flat, green farmlands, the bike strong and responsive on the gentle curves. He waved and smiled, passing the John Deere chugging along at 25 miles per hour.

*I wonder what Mama and Uncle Emile are doing now.* His uncle had seemed normal during his brief stay at home, but Mama had seemed worried and remote. To his queries of "Are you okay?" her answer was always, "Not to worry. I'm fine."

Miles later, as he rode past the Dells, hunger started to gnaw at his stomach. *Must remember to come back and visit here soon.* He pulled the bike off the side of the road next to a sign that pointed the way to Baraboo and Devil's Lake State Park. *Time to see what goodies Mama packed in that sack.* He found a loaf of her homemade sourdough, roasted chicken drumsticks, boiled farm-fresh eggs, Granny Smith apples, navel oranges, peeled carrot sticks, and still-warm blueberry muffins wrapped in aluminum foil. He washed down two boiled eggs, a chunk of bread, a carrot, and an apple with gulps of water from the bottle in his knapsack. "Thanks, Mama."

He relieved himself in the ditch and mounted the Harley. *Devil's Lake, huh?* And roared off in the direction the sign pointed. The park entrance was already crowded when he purchased an admission ticket. "Will you be camping? You will need to rent a campsite too."

"No thanks, I'll just be passing through." *Must watch the funds. I hope this is worth it.* Then, the hours were not long enough to explore and experience all the park offered: grand 500-foot rocky cliffs that overlooked the shimmering lake, miles of walking and climbing trails, shy white-tail deer in the woods, and turkey vultures high in the branches. Coyotes and foxes would not appear until near sunset. A park sign overlooking the lake noted, *Named "Tee Wakacah, Sacred Lake" by the native Ho Chunk tribe. Renamed Devil's Lake by the white man.*

As daylight dwindled, he found himself in the elevations of the Pygmy Forest, a stand of stunted ash and hickory trees. *Probably too late to get a camping permit. I suppose they're filled up, anyway.* He pulled the Harley off the road onto the soft green grass and hid it behind tall shrubs among the ancient 20-foot trees. The evening was still warm. *No campfire tonight and no tent to draw attention. Dinner time.*

After drum sticks and another chunk of sourdough, he peeled an orange for dessert with a muffin. The sun set. The sky was clear. He zipped up his jacket and lay on the soft earth next to the bike, the knapsack pillowing his head. Sleep came in moments to his trouble-free mind.

In the morning, he found the lake shore and shared it with a great blue heron standing proudly aloof while he swam in the cool water. He'd wait to have the last of Mama's muffins until he got coffee and gassed up outside the park.

In early afternoon, he meandered onto the interstate heading west to La Crosse where a mom-and-pop dinner of country fried steak, hash browns, salad, and pie sated his hunger for $10, including tip. Then he left Wisconsin behind, riding the slow lane into Minnesota, land of 10,000 lakes. That night, he opened his tent under the stars near the shores of the wide Mississippi.

The low-slung saddle of the Softail Slim began to feel like home as Morgan zig-zagged west across Minnesota on state and county highways, wherever the bike had a mind to go. He wandered as far north as Mankato, then headed southwest on U.S. 60, joining interstate 90 again near the southern border and on into South Dakota.

Morgan pulled into the Motel 6 at Sioux Falls. No camping out tonight. He needed a long soak in a hot shower to ease his muscles and remove the grime of the road. Judging by the map, he might have another all-day ride tomorrow, though he had no fixed destination in mind.

In the morning, he checked out and made his way to Denny's for breakfast—sausage, scrambled eggs, orange juice, and whole wheat toast. Against his better judgment, he ordered coffee too. A stimulant but a diuretic too. Waiting for his order, he studied the maps. South to Nebraska or North to North Dakota or continue west? *Almost 300 miles to the Badlands. 350 to Custer State Park. 400 to the Black Hills. I could make that in six hours if I rode without a break. More likely ten or more allowing for gawking and eating and pee breaks.*

Then he was on the bike again, heading west. At the Badlands, he wondered, *Is this still planet earth?* He idled the Harley while he took photographs of his surroundings, half expecting dinosaurs to appear in the stratified landscape dating back millions of years. Back on the road, he attached ear buds to the iPhone and listened to playlists of Wagner and Stravinsky, time and miles melting away, his mind often blank but for the music and the thrill of the ride.

In late afternoon, he encountered other motorcycles on the highway, more than he'd seen on the ride so far. When they left the interstate at Rapid City, he followed. Dark was approaching as he rode into Sturgis, amazed at streets jammed with bikes of every size, shape, color, and manufacture, unaware he was part of the largest motorcycle rally in the world. He pulled into the last available slot at the end of a long line of bikes, just beating out a rider on a Honda Goldwing trike with *Son of Satan* and a Swastika on the sides of his open-faced helmet. "Hey, Dipstick! I wanted that spot! How about you just back your ass out with that cute little bike and make room for a real biker?" The voice rose ominously over the roar of the Goldwing's angry revving engine.

Morgan quickly dismounted and made his way up the crowded street, ignoring the leather-vested trike rider, confident he couldn't be followed through the morass of machines. *Maybe that was a mistake, but the chances of meeting again will be remote ... I hope.* A sign under a streetlight announced: *Welcome to Sturgis—Campers Register Here.* He hadn't thought of where or how he would spend the night, but dark had descended. He had never ridden at night. Minutes later, he revved up the Harley and headed to Buffalo Chip campground on the outskirts of town.

Even more crowded than the streets he had come from, he passed tents and motorcycle camping trailers, vendors hawking biker goods and souvenirs emblazoned with *Sturgis 2007* and *Buffalo Chip*, a crowded swimming pool, concert stages, eateries, and a proliferation of bars. Still stunned by the scene, he found a place to park and pitched his small tent near a bathhouse and toilet.

Now he was hungry. Outside one of the bars, a low voice accosted him, a voice he had heard before. "Hey, Weasel, didn't you hear me before? I'm planning to rip your nuts off just for fun … if you have any, little man."

Morgan thought quickly. Plan A: I'm pretty sure I can outrun him. Plan B: Maybe I can kill him … with kindness. He grinned at Son of Satan, wondering if he should have accepted his uncle's offer of the pearl-handled pistol. *Then again, I wonder what it would take to bring this moose down.* Ignoring his own impending doom, he turned to face the irate biker. "You look like someone I could trust. You seem to know your way around. Can you give me some advice?"

Son of Satan stopped short in mid-stride, a blank stare of disbelief and confusion replacing the gratuitous hate in his eyes. Morgan gulped and continued, "Can I buy you a beer … if we can get to a bar? This place is crazy!"

Son of Satan raised a quizzical eyebrow. "Stay close, little man." And he bullied a path to the bar, elbowing, shoving and bulldozing the way. Morgan expanded on Plan B. "You're kinda handy to have around, big guy. Where you from, if you don't mind saying?"

The big man's brow wrinkled as if in deep thought. "Been on the road so much, I hardly recollect. Hills of Kentucky, I guess. But I left ... kicked out, really. Did the neighbor's daughter wrong. Hell, she was ugly. Spent some years on the wrestling circuit. Maybe you know me. Son of Satan?" He grinned proudly, displaying a mouthful of stained teeth. "Still got all my choppers see. Hey, where's that beer?"

Morgan shouted, "Barkeep! Two big drafts and two Kentucky bourbons ... make it doubles, for me and my friend."

Hours later, the barkeep informed them. "Bar's closed. Come back tomorrow."

"Okay. SOS, time for some shuteye." Morgan's words came slowly and slurred. He struggled to escape the big biker's embrace.

"Okay little buddy." Tears streamed down his face. "Hope I can find you tomorrow."

That was not Morgan's plan. *Not if I can help it.*

## Chapter 14
## Denise

The rumble and roar of motorcycle engines revving woke Morgan at dawn, bikers breaking camp, some moving on. He struggled to open his eyes. The scent of bacon frying at some distant campfire could not detract from the sharp ache that threatened to pop his eyeballs from his head. He stumbled toward the bathhouse, his bowels churning. Had he eaten last night? He could remember only shots and beer—more beer and whiskey than he had ever imbibed before—and his burly companion, Son of Satan.

A sign on the door announced a group ride today. Leaving at 10AM. Returning 3 PM. Experienced guide. Limit of 50 riders. $10. *Shit, I can afford that, but can I stand it?* He relieved himself and shuffled back to his tent.

Mama's sack of goodies still held a few pieces of fruit and the last remnant of sourdough. He abstained, fearful of putting food in his uneasy stomach. His guts moderated to merely queasy. Now, he needed coffee badly. The bar of last night's debacle had four tables set up outside and offered free coffee if you could stand on one leg for ten seconds. On the third try, he succeeded. No other customers appeared for the challenge. He took a seat at a round metal table.

A waitress dressed in leather short shorts and a low-cut tank top that read *Sturgis 2007* approached. A daisy tattoo with three missing petals decorated the top of her left breast. She leaned across the table, her long, tawny hair spilling forward. "Hey cowboy, what ran over you? You are one sorry sight."

"I did my one-leg stand. How about some fresh coffee? S'posed to be free."

"Just coffee? Okay. Yeah, it's free. Except for the tip." She winked. "Don't go away. I'll be back in a jiff." She returned with a carafe and two souvenir mugs. She poured two coffees and took a seat across the table from him. "No one else here at this early hour, so you have me all to yourself. Name's Denise. What's yours?"

The coffee washed most of the rat fur from his mouth and the throbbing from between his temples. "Uh, it's ... uh, Morgan." He glanced up at his uninvited guest. "Refill, please."

"Well, Mr. Morgan, at least we got your eyes opened ... big improvement. Sorta cute, aintcha."

"Not Mr. Morgan. Just Morgan."

"I see."

"Your shirt says Sturgis 2007. You live here?" He took another look at the daisy.

"No, but I've been here lots before. Come every year on my summer break to ride a little. Waitressing pays the tab. I live just outside Phoenix."

He wasn't really looking for conversation but eventually managed, "You waitress in Phoenix too?"

She laughed. "Hell no. I teach second grade. I'm married with two kids. Boy and girl."

"Your husband and kids are here, too?"

"Nope, just me. Mac, that's my husband, and I have a deal. I get a summer month off from family and kids every year. He takes care of the kids and the house. Then he does the same when and if he is free sometime in the winter. Poor guy hasn't had his month to do whatever he wants for two years, but I still got mine."

"Sounds like a great arrangement." He sipped the hot, black revival potion. "Bit odd though, isn't it?"

She flipped her hair. "I suppose some strait-laced numb-nuts might think so. My school principal sure doesn't know. What happens in Sturgis stays in Sturgis." She laughed, the sound of music.

"So, Denise, do you know anything about the group ride today?"

"Yeah, yeah. Great experience. I've done it twice before. Do you do group rides? You definitely want to do this one. I can sell you a ticket."

"Never rode in a group."

"Won't be a problem. Only fifty riders if it sells out. Always does. They will take it slow. Hit all the highlights nearby. Deadwood down to Needles highway. All that. Just a ride-by. I know the ride leader. Goes by the name Son of Satan, but don't let that worry you. That's only his name sometimes when he's here at the rally. Comes most every summer. Likes to act out different personas when he's here. Real name is Marvin Miller. Don't know if that's real either. He's an actor. Teaches theater at some community college in California."

*Son of Satan ... a fraud? An actor? Had me sweating.* He hesitated, then handed her a twenty, ten for the ticket and ten for the tip, too embarrassed to ask for change, though he was sorry to see the Jackson go. "Okay, one ticket, please."

She returned with his ticket attached to a yellow sticky note with her name and Arizona address on it. "This is so next time you're in Phoenix, you can look me and Mac up. Have a great ride, cowboy Morgan. Let me know later how it went."

"I'll do that. Thanks for your help, especially the coffee."

At 9:45, fifty eager riders assembled in 25 rows of pairs. Marvin Miller, aka Son of Satan, stood facing them from the back of his Honda trike, megaphone in hand. His swastika helmet was replaced by one resembling a spiked WWI German army helmet. He raised his hand to quiet the group. "Kill your engines, please. Listen up." Quiet settled over the anxious group.

"We'll be taking a slow, easy ride, often down to 15, 20 miles per hour. Only way to be safe on the hairpin curves and hills. If you're in a hurry, better drop out now." No one left.

"Always maintain two bike lengths between riders, front to back, side to side. Might get cozy through some of the tunnels. Don't break formation to gawk at the scenery. You'll be on your bikes for the whole ride except for Deadwood, our first and only stop. You will have 45 minutes there on your own to grab a quick lunch or a beer at one of the saloons ... maybe snap some photos of the old western architecture or the graves of Calamity Jane and Wild Bill at the cemetery. We will reassemble promptly in front of Saloon Number 10 and move out together.

"Heading south, I plan to ride past Mount Rushmore and the Crazy Horse Memorial. We will not stop in order to avoid parking fees. This is an orientation ride. We will keep moving slow and steady unless the four-wheelers or a herd of bison gets us tied up. You can return later to any of it on your own."

"Crank 'em up. Let's go." He handed the megaphone to an attendant.

At 10:02, the ground shook with the vibrations of fifty motorcycle engines starting as one. The air choked with exhaust, and the cheers of 50 bikers eager to be on the road with the summer wind in their faces, exploring the beauties and mysteries of the Black Hills. At 2:59, Morgan and 49 other riders followed Son of Satan, Marvin Miller, back into Buffalo Chip Campground, sated with scenery of Nature's grandeur and a bit of history of the early Wild West.

The unchanged streets of Deadwood easily recalled the old west town where liquor had flowed in a dozen saloons and tired whores lured their drunken clients upstairs for half an hour of relief from their difficult lives and where aces and eights became the dead man's hand of the legendary James Butler Hickok—Wild Bill. Absorbing the ambiance and history of the place left no time for even a quick bite, though he hadn't eaten for twenty-four hours.

Then on into nature's preserves—stands of subtly fragrant pine and spruce, quiet meadows where pronghorns grazed in tall grass surrounded by birch and aspen forests, rugged granite mountains, and needles of igneous rock that rose in the air like ancient church spires. Wildlife of Custer State Park: wapiti with miraculous racks and their high-pitched wild calls, bison herds grazing quietly on rolling hills, mule deer on the edge of the forest, and prairie dogs observing the passing parade, nervously conscious of the eagles and hawks soaring and floating high above.

And creations of men, the massive stone heads of four presidents carved into Mount Rushmore and the emerging head of Crazy Horse, the Oglala Lakota chief who led 3,000 or more warriors to defeat 200 soldiers of the United States Cavalry at the battle of the Little Big Horn, Custer's last stand.

Morgan's stomach growled, not from distress this time but from hunger. He was famished. During the ride, he had forgotten he'd had no nourishment but alcohol and coffee since lunch on the road yesterday. He headed toward the saloon to find food and tell Denise of his ride today. His cell phone chirped. 4:20 PM, who could be calling? The voice on the phone was hardly a whisper.

"Mama? Hi, Mama. How are you and Uncle Emile?"

"I hate calling you like this, Morgan. Are you having a good trip? Morgan, I'm frightened."

"My God! What happened?"

"It's Emile. He's confused and belligerent again. He punched me today, good and hard. He hauled off and hit me in the face! I'm so ashamed. He shouted, 'Get out of the way, whoever you are.' I am really scared, Morgan. I couldn't contact the doctor. What should I do?"

He did not hesitate to reply. "I'm coming home now, Mama. I'll leave right now and won't stop till I'm there. Be careful. Keep trying the doctor. Stay away from Uncle. I'm on my way, but it's almost 1000 miles. I'll stay on the interstates to make good time. Still, maybe twelve hours or more."

He packed up his tent and backpack in minutes. He would have to stop for gas somewhere. His hunger forgotten, he mounted the Harley and roared out of Buffalo Chip and Sturgis heading east, leaving Denise and Son of Satan behind, heading home.

He gassed up at a Loves in mid-state, neglecting to tend to his own body's needs. Mile after mile, doggedly pushing himself and the Harley, pushing toward home, impelled by Mama's voice—I'm frightened, Morgan! Almost thirty-six hours without food and little to no sleep, his body rebelled, insisting on rest and sustenance. His hands shook and his eyes refused to focus. He could no longer deny his body respite from hunger and fatigue. He staggered into a Loves Travel Center somewhere in eastern Minnesota, still hours before dawn. The *18-wheeler* chili seemed to have a diesel base. The thick, dark coffee tasted like yesterday's underwear, but he pointed for a refill. Before it arrived, his head hit the booth table, and he slept at last.

No one in the near-vacant truck stop bothered to wake him or even notice him. He revived three hours later, feeling refreshed, wondering where he was. The empty bowl and full cup of cold coffee remained before him. Recalling his mission, a sense of urgency returned. He dropped a ten next to the coffee and hurried out in the dark. A light rain had begun. That would make the roads dangerous. He mounted the Harley and resumed his flight home. Cautious of the rain and oil slick, he was forced to slow down. Still impatient, he pushed the bike beyond legal limits and pushed himself beyond what he had ever known possible, riding into the dawn. The scenery of Wisconsin's rolling hills welcomed him, and the rain stopped. He punched Mama's phone number. No answer. He rode north past waking cities, onto the familiar roads of Door County.

At eight in the morning, he burst into the farmhouse. Mama knelt in the kitchen sobbing, the pearl-handled automatic in her hand. Her beloved Emile lay on the floor, a dark stain forming around his head.

## Chapter 15
## Julia

Morgan dropped to his knees next to his dear aunt. She shook with sobs in his arms. "Mama, what happened here? Please stop crying. Tell me what happened."

Aunt Esther's words spurted sporadically between agonized wails and heart-wrenching sobs. Finally, Morgan understood the awful truth.

"I don't know how … he found it … the gun, his pistol. I hid it in my … chest of drawers. He never looks at my stuff."

Her tears streamed uncontrollably. She resisted Morgan's attempts to help her rise from the floor. She would not move from the side of her dead husband. "It's my fault. I killed him."

"Oh no, that can't be true."

"If I had locked it in the safe, he could not have found it. If I had watched him closer…. The last thing he said was, 'I'm sorry my love, I can't bear any more of it.' He raised the gun to his head. I tried to stop him. The awful noise … and he fell."

"Please, come sit in this chair while I call 911."

But, only the paramedics team was able to move her from Emile's side an hour later. "I'm very sorry Madam. We must be able to examine the body."

Morgan arranged for the cremation, as his uncle's will requested. It also specified that Esther would receive almost all of his assets, although, under Wisconsin law, she would do so automatically. Only the exceptions mattered.

> All of my earthly belongings shall go to my wife of more than 40 years, Esther Morel, with these exceptions: I bequeath $10,000 to my sister, Julia Morel, and $10,000 to my nephew, Morgan Morel, who will be executor of my will.

Morgan asked, "Who is Julia? Do I have a long-lost aunt?"

"You do, or did. She is Emile's older sister. Lived out east. Reclusive. She never replied to Emile's cards and letters at Christmas after he located her. Might not still be alive."

Morgan started to search for his unknown aunt with the P.O. Box address in Massachusetts Esther had given him. During the following week, he examined his uncle's financial records. He arranged for transfer of the Payable on Death brokerage and bank accounts into Esther's name and distribution of the $250,000 payout of a longstanding life insurance policy.

The county Medical Examiner had certified death caused by suicide. He informed his aunt that the term policy purchased just three months earlier with the same death benefit would pay nothing.

"I don't care. It won't bring Emile back to me. Morgan, have you been able to contact her, Emile's sister?"

"I used the address you gave me to discover a phone number for a Julia Morel. That must be her, but so far there's no answer whenever I call."

"Please try again … and, Morgan, with all this upset, I forgot the mail that came for you while you were out West. It came the day before you got back. It looks official."

Tears were never far from Esther's eyes. "I'm going to try to nap. Wake me to fix supper in an hour, please. I'm so sorry. I completely forgot until now." She handed him a business envelope and left the room.

He eagerly tore open the envelope from the Wisconsin Board of Bar Examiners and read.

### Official Notification of Suspension from the Wisconsin Bar.

We have not received your report filing of completed required Continuing Legal Education (CLE) activities. Your law license is, therefore, suspended for a period of two years on the condition you do complete acceptable continuing education courses within that time period. Until such time, you are prohibited from the practice of law in Wisconsin.

Please reply by mail with any questions.

Morgan's hurried reply stated that he had been accepted to the bar just months earlier, coincident with satisfactory completion of the Marquette University Law Scholars program. He noted that he did not require CLE credits at this time and for some time in the future and added

Please correct this apparent clerical error on your part and notify me of my renewed grant to practice law ASAP!

I can supply copies of any Marquette University documents you might require.

Signed Morgan Morel, Esq.

*I can't believe this. It's an obvious mistake. A horrible, fucking, damned mistake.*

Esther napped in what had been Emile's favorite La-Z Boy recliner in the family room. Morgan was reluctant to disturb her with still more bad news. Later, during dinner of grilled pork loin, sweet potatoes, canned green beans from last year's harvest, and a glass of Italian Chianti he told her his good news.

"I finally spoke with Emile's sister. She is coming here to visit and sign documentation for her inheritance. She seems eager to meet you and me. She didn't know of Emile's death or even that we existed, her only living kin. I hope you don't object to her staying here with us."

"I surely don't object. Maybe having someone else here to share my grief will be helpful."

His aunt retrieved a plain cremation urn from the sideboard and held it out. "What should I do with these ashes, Morgan?"

She seemed so utterly dejected. "I don't know, Mama, the will didn't have any suggestions. Did Uncle Emile ever talk about it with you?"

"Only that he loved it here in Wisconsin. This is where he would want to remain."

"Maybe Julia will have a suggestion. She'll be here next Monday. I'm picking her up at the airport at noon. You're welcome to ride along of course." He poured a third glass of Chianti.

"I think I'll stay here and continue to sort through his things. It's such a mournful task. Maybe his sister will help me with it then."

Morgan waited at the gate for the arrival of his aunt on the American Airlines flight from Boston. Among the deplaning passengers, he easily recognized her facial resemblance to his uncle. Julia Morel was a slight, wiry-appearing, gray-haired woman. He went to relieve her of the large carry-on bag she struggled with.

"Thank you, but I'm quite capable of toting my own luggage." She set the heavy bag down. "You're Morgan, I reckon. And I am your Aunt Julia. You may give me a hug."

He complied. "Welcome to Wisconsin, Aunt." He picked up her bag. "Can you walk to the parking lot?"

"Of course, I'm old, not an invalid." She linked her thin arm through his free arm. "Let's go."

"Do you have any more luggage?"

"No, that's it."

As they walked arm in arm, she chattered like an old, long-lost friend. "I want to know all about you and your parents ... and my brother Emile and his wife." Her voice rose with excitement. "I know we're going to be a loving family now, after all these years apart."

"Aunt Esther is having a difficult time with Emile's death, especially how he died. I know she will appreciate your visit and sharing the memories you both have of him." He marveled how comfortable he felt with this stranger almost instantly, how he had accepted her as if she had always belonged in his life. Yes, they shared ancestral genes, but something more drew him to her, something he did not understand and could not explain, but that he accepted without question.

~~~

The women sat together sipping afternoon tea. Morgan paced the wide farm-kitchen floor, absorbed in thought, catching occasional bits of conversation. Esther said, "You disappeared from the family almost fifty years ago. Then, Emile found you. But, why did you never reply to him when he reached out to you time after time?"

"I know now I should have, and I deeply regret I didn't. I was alone and reclusive for so long … so long with no family or no other being that cared. Maybe I didn't know how. Maybe I still did not want my family to know what had happened to me."

She sipped her tea, a look of nostalgia on her pensive face. "I was in love with a boy when I was just 17, still in high school. A sweet, darling boy. Enough to break your heart. I gave him all my love. I gave him everything."

"I was 23 when I met Emile and we married. I can understand."

"His name was Cecil. Cecil Brown. When I found I was pregnant, we planned to elope. I waited all night at the window for Cecil to come for me. He never came. I wanted to die."

Julia glanced away from Esther's searching eyes, her own brimming with tears.

"I travelled to Massachusetts alone, without my Cecil, just as we had planned to go together. For a time, I hoped he might decide to join me, but I never heard from him again. When I aborted the baby, it was like losing him one more time. I was young and afraid. I was ashamed. Then I was angry. Not just at Cecil. At the world."

She sat quietly for a moment, gazing into the past. "I took a job at the Law Library in Dartmouth and a room nearby. My love withered into bitter resentment." She smiled. "Oh, I had plenty of offers. College boys mostly. I treated them like dirt. Tease and retreat, never allowed a relationship to develop. Years went by. My family didn't know what had become of me. The offers eventually stopped too."

She wiped away a tear. Her face became stern, almost bitter.

"I spent 47 years at that library, moving up to assistant librarian and finally head librarian the last twelve years. I bought an old house on lonely Buzzards Bay and commuted half an hour every day, summer and winter. That's when I got a phone, but no one ever called. I didn't miss a day except one week with the flu. Emile found me there in 2000, just before I retired. He said he'd been searching for years during his sales travels in the Northeast. Then he never came again."

Esther said, "Emile retired in late 2001, and we came here to Wisconsin. He didn't travel anymore. Then we found Morgan about a year after that. I guess you were lost in the shuffle."

"I imagined he despised me until I got his first Christmas card a few years later."

The two women clasped hands. Esther said, "I'm so sorry we suffered all those empty years, but we're together now for however long. That makes me very happy, even though it took Emile's death to bring us together."

Julia's face shone, her eyes bright with joy and tears. She looked around the spacious kitchen. "Morgan, are you here? I didn't know I had another younger brother until Emile told me about Jules and your mother's death. That terrible accident. I thought maybe our parents named him Jules after their young daughter, who went away one day and never returned. Emile told me about you too and how grateful he and Esther were to have found you."

Morgan bent to hug his two aunts' shoulders. "When I first came to live here, that is what made my mom and dad's deaths bearable. Then, before long, Esther and Emile became my new parents … my second parents."

He sat with them at the table, hesitant to speak. "Mama, I can't set up my law office now as I'd planned." He explained the erroneous suspension details.

"But that's awful. What can we do?"

"I have already objected. Now I'll have to wait. How long? Who knows? Uncle's estate is settled, so I want to take the Harley on another little trip … if you and Julia are okay with that. I don't plan to be away long. Just trying to get my shit and my head together. I hoped Aunt Julia wouldn't mind staying awhile."

"Of course, Morgan. Go. Whatever you need." She turned to her new-found sister-in-law. "I'd love for you to stay with me if you can."

"Aunt Julia, what do you think?"

"Well, I don't have to get back home until early November to prepare the house for winter and make sure my half dozen lobster pots are out of the bay. But hurry back. I have much to learn about you yet, and we have so many years to make up."

# Chapter 16
# MacArthur

He had been on the road a day short of two weeks since leaving Mama and his Aunt Julia in Wisconsin. Fate alone or mere serendipity guided his travel. He loved the steady, reassuring hum of the Harley on long, straight hauls and the agile acceleration and maneuvering in traffic or on mountain curves. He angled across Wisconsin on US 151 before joining I80 in Iowa and following it west across Nebraska and Colorado. He camped out in his one-man tent or hosteled at convenient motels as the time and road dictated. Still worried, he called Mama every other day.

"Yes, yes. Julia and I are getting along fine. It's so nice to have female companionship for a change, especially at a time like this. We are finding a lot to share. I wish we had met like this years ago. Emile rarely spoke of his older sister, but she has much to tell about him … times before I knew him and times he hadn't ever spoken about." A long pause. "Are you okay?"

"I'm fine. Just wandering around. No idea how long I'll be gone. But if you need me, I'll be back in no time."

"Just enjoy your travels, dear boy. Julia and I are having a fine time together. She has decided to stay for a while. I'm very well pleased with that."

The days were mostly fair and sunny but cool enough for him to don his leathers for warmth and safety on the mountain roads of Colorado. He toured Avon, the ski town, and had lunch. He passed through Vail, unwilling to spend $50 to park the bike before entering the town. At dusk, he pulled into Glenwood Springs and spent the night at the historic Hotel Colorado where notables like Teddy Roosevelt and Al Capone had stayed and dined a century earlier.

In the morning, he turned south, out of the mountains, and camped that night in the desolate Painted Desert, reminiscent of the Badlands of South Dakota. Was that only months ago? He worried, *What if the suspension holds? What if they don't correct their mistakes ever? It's been weeks since I sent my letter objecting to their error, and still no response.*

Cell phone reception was too weak to hear Mama's reply when he asked if there had been any mail from the Wisconsin BBE. He took a long draft of Glen Livet from the bottle in his backpack. *I can't just tour around the country for years. I need something to do.*

At Flagstaff, he spent a day touring around the Grand Canyon. In the evening, he was lucky to find a room at the popular El Tovar Hotel, another favorite of Roosevelt, as well as Einstein and Zane Gray. It had been a long day. He lingered in the soothing comfort of the hot shower. Digging into the depths of his knapsack for a change of underwear, he came up with two Buffalo Chip campground admission ticket stubs and a scrap of crumpled yellow paper. He unfolded the paper, the sticky note Denise had handed him in Sturgis. *Forgot all about this.*

He pulled up Google Maps and mused, "I can head directly south and be in Phoenix in a few hours. I wonder what the school teacher-bar tender is like at home."

In the morning, he rode leisurely through the shaded and scented National Forest lands. He was awed by the beauty of the red and white sandstone and basalt cliffs around Sedona and explored the surrounding byways for hours, finally moving south again after a late lunch.

Now, with the sun low on the horizon, he followed his GPS to the address scrawled on Denise's note. He rolled past a strip mall, two gas stations and a two story, pale adobe building labeled Community Center, then through neighborhoods of small bungalows, ranch homes and adobes. He found the address, a wide ranch with a lawn of cacti and dark landscape rock.

He pulled in and parked the bike next to a pink Harley Davidson on one side of the double driveway. A black-and-white with the letters CHPD and a police badge on the front doors occupied the other side of the drive. *Trouble in paradise?*

A small basketball goal stood at the end of the drive. A child's bicycle lay across the walk to the front door. He hesitated. *What if this is just her little prank? But, she did say she had two kids.* He rang the doorbell and knocked three times. Voices within.

The door opened. A pair of four-year-olds looked up into his eyes. The one he guessed was a girl had Denise's tawny hair but cropped short. The boy's head was covered with a mass of dark curls. In unison, the children shouted, "Mama, Daddy. It's for you."

Moments later, Denise waddled into view and approached the door. "Cowboy Morgan! Be damned. Didn't really expect to see you again after you stood me up in Sturgis. Come in. My God, come in. Thanks kids, go up to your room to play. Call Daddy first. Tell him we have a visitor."

She threw her arms around Morgan's neck. As they hugged, he became acutely aware of her large protruding baby bump. "Yeah," she said, "another one on the way. Hope it's not twins, again." She held her belly in both hands and laughed. "Oh, here comes Mac."

Douglas MacArthur appeared in a police uniform, captain's bars on his collar. Glancing at Denise, he asked, "Who do we have here?" His handshake was firm and vigorous.

"I met this cowboy in Sturgis in August. Didn't expect to ever see him again. His name is Morgan. Isn't he cute? Hey, Morgan, you never came back to tell me about your group ride. How come?"

As Morgan explained his hurried departure from Sturgis and his uncle's tragic death, Denise herded the two men into a small living room. "You two get to know each other while I put supper on the table. Cowboy, you will be staying to eat. It's just tacos and beans. The kids love them." She disappeared into the kitchen without hearing Morgan's objection.

"No, I just stopped by. I don't want to intrude. Just—"

"No use objecting," his host interjected, "She always gets her way."

They settled back on facing stuffed chairs, and silence settled on the room. Morgan spoke momentarily. "She told me about your arrangement ... where you each take a month off every year from your jobs and family."

"Yeah, we're a great team. Douglas and Denise ... double Dees. Don't guess that little arrangement will work this year with the new baby due about when I would be taking off somewhere. Also, we are very short-handed on the force, so I can't get away then anyway."

"Well, you're apparently a cop."

"How'd you guess? You would make a good detective." Mac laughed. "I'm not usually in uniform at dinner time, but I have to go back to the station for a few hours tonight. I'm the captain in charge of our small force, and have to fill in as needed."

"So, little old Cactus Hills has a police force?"

"Small one, to be sure. Just six of us now. We're far enough from Phoenix that our crime rate is very low. We have only three traffic lights. It's a peaceful community, and they support us. We have two cruisers. I drive one. One is on patrol 24/7 with a single police man or woman on eight-hour shifts. We continue to put one patrolman on the streets during daylight hours."

The captain continued, seeming pleased to share a subject dear to him. "Our community likes that and wants that, so we do it, though it's not common most places. Old Harvey's been making the rounds for years, but I really need some relief for him now."

He paused, seeming perplexed by his manpower problems. "The desk sergeant and I take care of headquarters. It's an old converted gas station. Maybe you saw it coming in. Got a detective too, but he just quit. I need to replace him and add to our foot patrol, so we're really up the manpower creek."

His frown morphed into a wry smile. "Don't suppose you're looking for work?"

Morgan laughed. "Not really, although I sorta am without a current active occupation."

Denise yelled from the kitchen. "Guys, kids, wash up. Come and get it. We're using the dining room tonight."

The small family and their unexpected guest gathered around the table set with two lighted tapers, wine glasses, water goblets, milk glasses for the children and colorful paper plates.

Douglas remarked, "Wow, all out, Hon."

"Well, the kitchen is too crowded. Morgan, these are the twins, David and Danielle. They're four. Dani and David, say hello to Mr. Morgan."

The twins, in unison, "Hello, Mr. Morgan."

"No, Morgan is my first name, remember. My last name is Morel."

Mac remarked, "Morel, like the mushroom?"

Morgan frowned. "Exactly."

Denise urged them, "Eat now, before it gets cold."

She poured red wine for the two men and water for herself. "Sorry I can't join you now."

Morgan took a hungry bite. "These are the best tacos I've ever had. How do you get the shells so tasty?"

"I just use tortillas from the store and heat them in a pan with a little oil." Denise almost blushed.

"That your Harley Sportster our front?" Morgan asked. "Can't feature Mac doing his police rounds on it."

"That's mine alright, my ride to Sturgis or wherever my fancy takes me." She pointed down with her forefinger. "I took Junior for a ride this morning, but I think I'll have to put it up for the duration."

Mac laughed. "I'll park it in the garage for you later ... if I can find room enough. By the way, Honey, Morgan said he doesn't have a job. I told him we could use him on the force."

Denise asked, "Didn't you tell me something about being a lawyer, Morgan?"

Morgan explained the situation of his mistaken suspension by the Wisconsin Board of Bar Examiners. "I don't know when or how it will be resolved. Damned frustrating, and it seems there is nothing more I can do about it."

Mac offered, "Well, with your knowledge of the law, you're already more qualified than any other new cadet at the academy. I could qualify you personally in a week or so, including a day of weapons training on the range. We're pretty much able to make our own rules here in Cactus Hills. No one looking over our shoulders."

The wine and the meal had Morgan feeling mellow. *Why not? Mama's fine. I've got nothing but time and nowhere to go. Maybe, I'll get a look at some real crime.* He'd had enough for now of roaming the country on the Harley. He looked at Douglas. "It might be very short term. Can't commit to stay if anything develops in Wisconsin. A year, maybe two at the absolute most."

Mac raised his glass of Shiraz and grinned. "I'm thinking your showing up on our doorstep just now was a very lucky coincidence for all of us. Welcome to the CHPD and $24 per hour."

With Mac's personal instructions and his eagerness to fill at least one staff position with a warm body, a crash orientation in procedures from Diego Aguilar, the desk sergeant, and Morgan's bright and eager learning, the usual academy training was shrunk to twelve hectic days. He learned patrol operations, traffic control, defensive tactics, and a smattering of investigative techniques. Mac certified his qualifications hoping the state police board was still too busy to monitor his small force.

Two uniforms arrived by Fed Ex the day his cram course in police work was completed. He stripped down to his shorts and removed his well-worn Skechers. He pulled on the dark navy pants, then the short-sleeved matching shirt with *Morel* stitched over the right pocket and CHPD patches on both arms. He ran the wide, black leather belt through the waist loops without attaching the holster or handcuff case included in the shipment, thinking *this is feeling really unreal.* He pulled up the black half-calf compression stockings and laced up the shiny black dress oxfords.

The black clip-on tie was next. Thank God for the clip-on, he'd never tied a tie. He straightened the police hat on his head, pulled down the stiff patent leather bill, and stood, stunned by his transformed image in the full-length mirror. *Damn, you could have fooled me. Maybe it will fool the good and bad citizens of Cactus Hills to believe this is a real cop.*

Monday morning, he signed out the rest of his standard issue equipment with Sergeant Aguilar—cuffs, baton, two-way radio and the Glock 22. He was ready to join the force and meet his fellow officers. He hoped they wouldn't laugh.

## Chapter 17
## Cactus Hills P.D.

The Cactus Hills Police Department was a disparate yet entirely cohesive group of distinct individuals that Morgan came to know in just the first few weeks on the job. Some greeted him warmly as a new and desperately needed member of the team. Others remained more aloof, even viewing his appearance in uniform askance or with marginal disdain.

Ana Alvarez, an attractive thirty-something, divorced and apparently available, shook his hand but restrained herself from a welcoming hug. She drove one of the patrol cars eight hours a day, alternating shifts with Lenny Silvers and Tony Campanelli, the other two patrol car drivers.

Lenny was 45 and married, no kids, lived in Cave Creek with his young wife, and commuted 33 miles day or night to report to the station house. How many times had the captain lectured him when he'd forgotten it at home that the visored cap was part of his police uniform to be worn at all times on duty. And shine up your shoes and leathers now and then. He extended a hand to Morgan. "Welcome to the CHPD. Captain Mac spoke highly of you. I hope you don't have any hobbies."

Tony was a bachelor, trim, muscular, and well-groomed. His crisp uniform was tailored to accentuate his build. He had never shown an interest in Ana's not-too-subtle overtures. The two, always in close contact on the job, rarely spoke except to exchange cruise information while changing shifts. Tony welcomed Morgan with reserved curiosity. "Hello, Morgan. Is there a Mrs. Morel?"

The three officers, spelled by Captain Mac, kept one of the two department Black and Whites cruising the streets of Cactus Hills at least 20 out of 24 hours every day, seven days a week. Citizens knew they could call at any time for an emergency jump-start or help with a flat. It was often the only action the patrols might encounter during a shift, and it was a welcome source of occasional tips to augment their limited salaries. Bribes to escape the speeding ticket fines that provided significant revenue for the department were, on the other hand, flatly refused.

Harvey Harris had endured two gang initiation beatings before he fled Chicago's south side with the girl he hoped to marry. His was one of only three black families residing in Cactus Hills. Not that the community was exclusive. Most residents were medium to high income and all but a very few lived modestly in conventional housing. An occasional BMW, Mercedes, or Lincoln Town Car was parked in driveways of the town's unassuming homes. Ford or Chevy pickups or family sedans and SUVs of Japanese or Korean heritage were more common.

Private Harris, known as Fats or more obliquely as Domino by his fellow cops, walked the beat that eventually covered most of the residential and commercial streets of the town. "Been walkin' the beat by myself for most of ten years," Harvey said when Morgan joined him on his rounds for training. "Good to have company again, though company never does last long. Few weeks, you'll be on your own. Cap'n's plan is we split the beat two ways soon as you learn the ropes."

"Ten years and still a private? Did you ever ask for reassignment or promotion?"

"Just grateful for what I got. See, I have a little trouble passing the annual agility and endurance tests. Cap'n Mac fudges the data sometimes or grants me an exception. But he keeps me walkin' the beat for my own good. Says, long as my BP stays under 150, I'll have a job."

"All that walking should keep your weight down and your BP too."

"It's a matter of calories in versus calories out. Martha, that's my wife, she's a great cook. Not too calorie-conscious, especially when it comes to pasta and beans and three-layer cakes. She ain't happy if I don't eat what she feeds me when I get home. Love that woman."

Morgan learned that the small businesses that occupied the strip mall were anchored by grocery and office supply chains plus McKlean dry cleaning, Bob the Barber, The Great Wall Chinese, a taco joint, the ubiquitous pizza place, and the coffee house. Whatever the varied route their foot patrol took, barring some unusual delay that required police attention, it invariably led to The Brew House within minutes of 10AM.

"Morning, officers. Good to see you again today." Mable, the sixty-something waitress, set two mugs of coffee on the counter, Morgan's black, Harvey's with mocha and cream. She returned with two filled donuts for Officer Harris. "Your usual, Harvey." Turning to Morgan, she winked. "Nothing for you, honey? No charge for our faithful guardians in blue."

"Thanks, no. Thanks for the coffee." And he left a dollar tip for her.

After the second week of making rounds together, Harvey and Morgan split the beat, allowing them to cover almost half the town every day. And every day, they rendezvoused at the Brew House to exchange notes. The coffee was always fresh. The conversation was routine and stale. Crime was on vacation in Cactus Hills.

"Martha says she wants to meet you. She's fixin' barbeque chicken skewers, chicken livers, greens and bacon, smothered potatoes and onions, and some special dessert. You're coming home with me tonight." Riding home later, so sated he struggled to stay awake, Morgan understood Harvey's love for his wife and the impossibility of his ever losing weight.

Desk Sergeant Diego Aguilar at 60 was the oldest member by far of the small police force. Diego took no crap when daily and weekly reports were not submitted promptly. He still would have preferred the paper filings of earlier years but kept a vigilant eye on the computer monitor and the CHPD.net website that served the force now. No problem for Morgan, whose reports were succinct and uneventful.

Walked quadrant A route, 7.5 miles. Coordinated with Pvt. Harris covering quadrant C. No problems observed. End of report.

Twice, his reports included interventions at family disturbances where he placated the warring partners with compassionate, practical advice before violence erupted. Once, a stray family dog returned to its owners. Once, a three-year-old little girl, a tom-boy in training, was rescued from a raft on the park pond and placed in the arms of her grateful, distraught parents. The *Hills News* ran an article with photos on page three.

He'd pulled his police automatic just once, nervously firing a warning shot over the heads of a group of three knife-menacing Latinos he'd interrupted in the process of stripping the wheels from a BMW in broad daylight. "Probably one of the gangs out of Phoenix," Aguilar noted indifferently. "They don't often bother us here."

Denise invited him often for dinner or a visit on his days off, though Douglas discouraged that in order not to show favoritism. Sipping a brandy with his benefactor and superior officer on one such occasion, Morgan screwed up his courage to speak his dissatisfaction. "I am grateful that you managed to place me in this job, Mac, but I can't take much more of this dullsville. I'm withering away on the vine. I need to get ahold of something with purpose, bite into it, taste it." He stood to face his host. "I think I'll have to leave the force."

MacArthur threw a dismayed glance in his direction. "Do you have something else, some other offers?"

"No. I could return to Wisconsin and try to settle things there. No reply from the BBE yet." Morgan's resolve weakened seeing Mac's deep distress. "But I'll give you whatever notice you need … three weeks … four."

Mac drained his snifter and set it on the end table. "I might have something better for you. With your knack for dealing with people and knowledge for the law, you're a natural for police work. Not everyone has that. I still need to replace my detective, and I have a new recruit coming next week who can take over your beat with Harvey. Would you be interested in investigative work? It's a better fit for you than the beat. There's even fifty dollars a month pay increase."

This was a possibility he had not considered, another benefit of being part of the small force commanded by his friend and mentor in law enforcement perhaps. "Well, I have learned a lot about law enforcement on the beat this past year. I've always had an interest in detective work. Studied criminal cases and crime scene investigations in law school as a hobby. But I don't have formal training ... forensic science, for example. And is there anything to investigate in Cactus Hills?"

"There are online courses, if you feel you need that here. Our budget can cover the cost. We have more to investigate than you might think. The cruisers report a lot you haven't been exposed to, admittedly mostly routine. Thefts, fights, beatings, property damage, the occasional missing person ... enough to keep you busy if not excited. We have a backlog of work. And we get requests for help on cases from neighboring forces and Maricopa County now and then."

"I will admit, I am interested in giving it a try. I have the curiosity and maybe the confidence. And, it has to be better than the beat. But when would I start?"

"Is tomorrow too soon? There has not been an applicant for the job in almost a year. I can really give the job to anyone I think is fit, and I think you're a fit for the needs of the CHPD."

"Give me one day off to think about it."

In the morning, Morgan took his blues to McKlean to be cleaned and pressed. He would hang them away with no intention of wearing them again. He drove the Harley to Mesa to purchase a proper detective's basic wardrobe—three pale blue button-down dress shirts, an ugly paisley tie, and two inconspicuous gray suits off the rack. Sergeant Aguilar supplied a shoulder holster and .32 automatic.

"Suppose you heard you're getting a new partner, Harvey, and I'll be trying out the detective job. I want you to know how much I appreciate everything you have taught me over these past months."

"Like I said, company never does last long. But you deserve more that the beat." He shoved out a black paw, then pulled Morgan into a bone-crushing bear hug. "Martha would sure love to fix a nice dinner for you again sometime. And maybe old Mable at the Brew House will still give you a free mug even though you ain't wearing the blues no more. I think she has a thing for you."

"I'll be sure to stop in when I have time, Harvey. Ten AM, right?"

But, when ten AM came, he never had the time.

## Chapter 18
## Monster

Two little faces laughed and smiled at Bowie Masters from the rear window of a school bus. "Hey, Rug Rats!" Bowie grinned and waved through the cracked windshield of his aged and rusted pickup, the 1990 Ford 150 he had acquired ten years ago, courtesy of Big John. The stenciled sign on the doors now read *Masters Construction* with a blacked-out blank space where Johnson's name had once been, and underneath, in small letters, *We Fix Their Mistakes.*

He liked kids. They had never betrayed him as the important adults in his life had. And children liked him, trusted him instinctively, smiled at him in passing, even instigated small conversations. They didn't find anything menacing about him.

Not so with the rare adults who ventured to know him better. Although his lined face appeared open and cheerful to a casual glance, up close, he triggered a sense of coldness, even menace, for some. Maybe it was the eyes, shaded under the frayed bill of his sweat-stained baseball cap. Maybe they found the pain they saw deep within too much to tolerate.

He felt good today. The stress and tension that had nagged him from the loss of his partner and mentor and the trials of a crumbling business were lifted for the time being. After Lee Roy Johnson died unexpectedly, leaving his home and all his belongings to his young protégé, the lucrative construction business they had operated together suddenly turned very sour. He felt helpless and abandoned, attempting to deal with misfortunes beyond his control.

First, ICE stepped up its arrests and deportations of illegals, sending one of his Mexican workers and his family home across the border. The rest of his crew went into hiding. Then, the housing bubble that had brought more work than they could handle burst. Cheap credit and easy mortgage loans disappeared. Masters and Johnson Construction went bust without a business, and a labor crew became redundant.

But today, he had been paid well for completion of two small repair jobs, and a week ago, a larger job at the fine home of Mr. Dale Grunwald, manager of the TruFont Hotel in Mesa, opened a new opportunity for him. "I like your work, Masters. Come see me at the hotel about some renovations there if you're interested."

That had landed a contract for at least three months of work. He might even be able to afford an assistant go-fer. Plenty of men were looking for anything they could get.

The bus turned off, but Masters continued, smiling, flooded with a rare sense of well-being and peaceful solitude. He drove with no real destination in mind, somewhere in the suburbs where most of his work was located, searching for residences that might need his services. He was unaware of his exact location until the approaching intersection stirred some vague, disturbing recollection and recognition—a small strip mall with an American Collateral Bank and Francisco's Southwest Grill, Laurie's Lingerie, and sundry other small businesses.

Why did these ordinary scenes provoke desperate, unreasonable fear? What was the repressed memory of some ominous act that struggled to be recalled? Then, the red, white and blue badges warning that the interstate was near.

An irresistible compulsion to flee, to escape the troublesome scene, grasped him. He jammed the wheel to the right, ignoring the blaring of horns and the screeching of brakes around him. The pickup shuddered as he jammed the accelerator and hit the on-ramp doing 50. His smile and inner tranquility were now gone—pushed suddenly and brutally aside by feelings of panic and remorse.

He frowned and squinted cautiously in his rearview mirror. *What's there? Is something back there?* A dull headache crossed his forehead. He relaxed his tight grip on the wheel, seeking to will his inner peace to return, hoping the headache would not turn into what he had come to call the bloody, black monster. It could disable him with pain. And it visited him more frequently now.

When it came without warning to possess him, he'd been powerless to resist its grip. He could not defray or delay the crippling, controlling pain. He would have tried or done anything—anything for relief. But he could not remember what enabled his escape from the crushing pain. He would have bartered his soul to be rid of it. Perhaps he had.

Memory was like a heavy black shroud, unyielding to his mental probes, deforming but not opening to reveal its contents. *What are you? Where are you from? What do you want from me?* Yet, he resisted stripping back the shroud lest the bloody black monster might emerge.

Fear enslaved him, fear of the pain that threatened to crush his temples when the monster seized his head. That is when he begged for release, before the darkness descended where memory could not reach, and the blood-red veil of unbearable pain blinded his eyes after— after what? When consciousness returned, he knew only that the pain was gone and something was very wrong.

Now, driving west on the interstate, the bright sun attacked his eyes. His thoughts leapt back into a bright summer day, Little League, late afternoon, retreating back, back, back into left field chasing the high fly ball, then the blinding sun in his eyes, the ball falling, not fielded, at his feet.

"I did try, Mama!"

"You should have had it, Bows. I came to watch a winner, not a loser."

"But … the sun, Mama."

He thought back to earlier days of comfort and pleasure when his mother had cared for her young son, bathing and grooming him, cutting his chestnut hair, sitting together to watch Barney and Baby Boo on television. Then, the closeness shuddered to an end before he was six, replaced by ridicule and neglect, and he could not understand. There was no pleasing Mama, no matter how he tried. What had he done wrong?

And nowhere to turn. Daddy whimpering, unable to defend himself from Mama's disdain. "Can't you get a better job? Can't we move out of this shit hole to a better place? Can't you stay sober and awake to take the kid off my hands while I go out for some fun? I want to go back to work. I want to be with other people. I want to be out of here. I want to be me." And when she left, Mory turned to the bottle, not to his needy son. Bowie was alone.

He knew the monster was with him now, in the truck. He swerved sharply, setting off a dissonant chorus of automobile horns while he crossed two lanes of traffic, seeking the nearest off-ramp. *Just let me find a place to park and rest a little.*

He eased the truck into a corner slot near the exit of an unfamiliar strip mall. His flannel shirt was drenched with sweat. He cranked down the truck window and waited, weary, his head resting on the steering wheel. Long shadows of late afternoon softened and faded into the dim light of dusk. He shivered with a cold fear while he raised his eyes and watched the steady flow of vehicles to and from the parking lot and customers entering and exiting the mall shops.

It touched him now. He'd known it would.

Bowie stepped down from the truck. Ferocious pain took command of his mind and body. He reached behind the seat to retrieve the long, black leather case and slid the zipper open. He held the Model 70 Winchester close to his side, returning to the driver's seat. Pain pressed his temples, momentarily blinding him. He blinked, leveled the rifle barrel out of the open window, and mumbled a promise of appeasement. "I'll do it."

He selected a convenient human target in the rifle's scope. He steadied his hand and squeezed the trigger.

One deadly round bore through the victim's head. A lone woman in a colorful floral dress paused before a brightly lighted storefront window, crumpled to the ground. Startled passersby gawked, some finally rushing to her still body, kneeling at her side.

Bowie carefully pulled back the bolt and caught the ejected cartridge. He put the truck in gear, calmly exited the mall parking lot, and slowly pulled away into the stream of evening traffic.

The monster whispered, "Good boy."

Bowie laughed with relief while hot tears fell from his eyes.

## Chapter 19
## Rhonda & Rose

When Maria and Mateo Rodriguez were blessed with their youngest set of twins, their oldest twins, Vanessa and Violeta, eighteen, knew it was time to leave their parents' home and make some kind of life for themselves. With seven remaining siblings to be housed, fed, clothed, and educated, the tiny house in the tiny Mexican town of Islita would be burgeoned beyond their parents' ability to cope.

The family's only livelihood came from selling "authentic" Mexican earthenware, woven goods, trinkets, fresh produce, and tasty beef empanadas to American tourists at the border. The authentic Mexican goods came from China and the Philippines. The produce came from Mateo's small garden, and Maria prepared the empanadas fresh daily at dawn before turning her attention to her brood of small, hungry children.

Vanessa and Violeta attracted customers to the small family vendor kiosk in the San Luis Rio Colorado border town by chattering with passersby in near-perfect English they had learned from the American tourists since they were four years old. Now, in their teens, their dark beauty also served as a magnet for many male customers. For this, Mateo was both thankful and wary.

They appealed to their older brother, Ernesto, who offered to deliver them safely across the border into America. He agreed to take them to Phoenix, Arizona. There would be no fees that he usually charged for transporting undocumented immigrants across the border. They agreed in unison, without hesitation, without knowing what America and the future had in store for them.

Mateo kissed his beautiful daughters with tears brimming in his eyes. "Adios mis queridas hijas. Adios. Do not forget your father and mother. Do not forget your family." The few hundred American dollars he handed each of them may have seemed much too little to send them on their uncertain way, but it was all he had. He pressed small gold crosses into their hands. "Adios, go with God," and he could no longer contain the tears that flowed from his dark and weary eyes.

~~~

Vanessa's hand trembled as she signed the guest register at the TruFont Hotel. Tired, hungry, and thirsty, she and Violeta had had neither food nor drink that day. Now they registered—as Ernesto had instructed before he disappeared—as Rhonda and Rose Rogers. "You must have a new identity here and new American names."

They were alone and on their own in the strange, vast new land of opportunity. Their only luggage, two flimsy cardboard suitcases, contained all the belongings they could bring to America.

The desk clerk offered, "Can I help take your luggage to your room?"

"No gra ... thank you." Bewildered and very hungry, Violeta asked, "But is there somewhere near to get a little food and drink?"

"Oh, yeah. See Jo-Jo in the bar. Limited food menu, but he can fix you up."

Jo-Jo, Joseph Minelli, had retired from the ring after ten years of middle-weight matches that had left a few scars on his broad face and his mind. He moved and talked a little slower now. He had bounced at several nightclubs in town and learned how to make the biggest and boldest wince with pain. Yet his wife and teen daughters knew him to be the gentlest man on earth.

Answering the help wanted ad for a bartender at the TruFont he had admitted his lack of mixology experience. Grunwald, the hotel manager, noted his bouncing experience. He looked him up and down and decided his bulky appearance behind the bar might tend to dissuade unruly customers from causing much trouble, and most of the TruFont clients drank beer. Minelli assured him that if a few words of warning were not enough, his firm hand on their arm or a moderated kidney punch would almost always be sufficient inducement for a quiet departure—after he collected their tab.

Jo-Jo watched the two young women cautiously enter the bar room. "Welcome, ladies. What'll it be?"

"We are hungry. Is there food here?"

"We feature an international selection from the microwave. Cheeseburgers ... plain or works, tacos and burritos, pizza ... cheese or pepperoni. Sorry, no Chinese. Five bucks each. What's your pleasure?"

Uncertain of what they might receive, they responded in unison to the first word they heard, "Cheeseburgers."

"With the works?"

Not wanting to reveal their ignorance, "Si, the works. But what is bucks? We have only dollars to pay."

Jo-Jo assured them, "Dollars are fine. Grab a seat in one of the booths. I'll deliver them when they're hot. Drinks?" He waved a hand at the back bar.

"Agua … water, please."

~~~

In their first letter to Maria weeks later, Rose described the many attractions of the city in America, the fine hotels to live in, fine restaurants to eat it, fine jobs for young women. She explained that she and Vanessa had new names to use in their new country, but they would always be Vanessa and Violeta Rodriguez in their hearts.

*You must not worry about us,* she wrote. *We both easily found employment as post office clerks and have plenty of money. We will be able to send American dollars home to you and Papa.*

In truth, without green cards, it was impossible to find jobs in the strange city. When they explained they could no longer afford the hotel room charges, Mr. Grunwald suggested a possible solution. "Suppose you keep the hotel rooms cleaned and made up. You know … hotel maids. And you are both lovely young women … women I'm sure many of our hotel patrons would appreciate knowing. Just be friendly with our male guests, make them feel welcome at the bar. Flirt a little. Flash those dark eyes. Have a drink with them. Maybe entertain them in their rooms when they are lonely?" He steepled his fingers together and peered over them quizzically. "Maybe your rent could be free."

~~~

The sisters sat facing each other in their usual booth in the TruFont barroom, a chess board on the tabletop between them. The afternoon sun filtered through the darkened window, casting long shadows from the chessmen. Rose said, "Checkmate … in four moves. You must not be here. Take the night off." She began collecting the pieces from the board. "You can't work tonight and no one will want you looking so pale and weak. Go up to the room. Sleep."

Back-to-back Rose stood a small inch taller than her sister. She left her long, dark hair hanging loose to her shoulders to cover the mole under her left ear, the distinguishing mark they did not share. Both women wore light clothing that clung just right to show off their full, shapely bodies—clothing easily removed and replaced. Rhonda enjoyed the freedom of close-cropped hair. Her smile was just a bit broader and brighter than her twin sister's, but her smile was lacking now.

She demurred Rose's suggestion but finally had to agree she would not be a suitable companion tonight for anything more than a quick blow-job or an evening watching television porn. "Okay, Roselita. I'm sorry, but I do feel like shit, and I guess it shows. It's Tuesday, though. Should be a slow night. Maybe you can take the night off too."

The abortion that morning, her third, had cost $1500. At least this "doctor" had not demanded a quickie before performing his work. There was the clinic for half the price, but they asked too many questions and offered too much advice. The pill worked, too, but was not recommended if you wore an IUD—useless damned things.

The women's clientele varied from steady customers to occasional lonely business men away from home. Some nights involved only accepting watered-down drinks for which their male companion paid elevated prices. Some nights meant an hour or two in an upstairs room. Grunwald left setting their rates and collecting their fees up to the women, but $50 went into the hotel cash register for each use of a hotel room.

Their subtle fear of violence never diminished, though Jo-Jo was always available if a John turned nasty or rough or unwilling to pay. Their customers—they called them companions—always left satisfied. Every morning, they lit candles at the chapel for the Blessed Virgin.

"Do you think we can ever move on, Roselita, to live a normal life with a home and kids? It has been six years since we escaped to a good life here from a better one at home. Will we ever escape the fucking TruFont hotel?" Pain wrenched her gut. "I'm going now. Jo-Jo will look after you, but call my cell if you need me."

## Chapter 20
## The TruFont Hotel

Bowie's contract for renovations at the TruFont included installation of new hotel room doors and replacing all the sash windows with double-pane fixed windows. The hotel's insurance deemed these security measures required to reduce the hotel's liability since several of the key lock doors had been broken into and vandalized.

The hotel security could have been considered lax. None of its short-term clients bothered to sign the desk register for an hour or so to stay with Rhonda or Rose. And now there was the unfortunate suicide leap from one of the third-floor room windows just a month ago.

Dale Grunwald, hotel manager, had ordered thirty electronically keyed doors and hardware. It was Bowie's task to measure the individual windows and order correctly sized replacements. Doors and windows completed, the bar room would receive new tongue-in-groove laminate flooring, a purely aesthetic measure. The contract included a $500 bonus to complete all the work in six weeks. Work in the bar room, a profit center for the hotel, would need to be done between 3AM Sunday and noon Monday.

To save time, he ate lunch on the job, lunches Josephina prepared for him and packed in brown paper bags—cold meat sandwiches or leftover cold chicken from last night's dinner, and a thermos of thin soup. He'd asked the old woman to stay on as cook and housekeeper, offering only room and board as compensation until his business improved. She seemed delighted to accept this and suggested to Bowie that this might be her retirement home. "I'm almost seventy, you know."

"You have a home with me as long as I have a home." He paid her a small, irregular salary when his own income allowed. She accepted without counting or comment.

Working alone, the job would demand Bowie's full-time, dedicated attention for the duration, but he decided hiring a grunt to assist him would have cut into his profit too much. The majority of the hotel rooms were unoccupied during the day. He could remain cloistered in them on the job nine or ten hours a day without interruption. Unless muscle pains from constant exertion or the unpredictable headaches plagued him, he rested rarely and then not for long. Then he might sprawl on the hotel bed a few minutes, a barely therapeutic activity. *These beds need replacing more than the doors and windows.*

He learned later that only a few of the rooms were reserved for travelers who might need to get a good night's sleep. Pushing the bed away from the window to allow himself more work space, a glitter on the floor where the bed had covered caught his eye—a set of keys.

Leaving after finishing the day's work, he tossed the keys to the desk clerk. "Found these."

"What room were they in?"

"Pretty sure it was 303. Yeah, it was 303."

"Oh, the suicide room. We haven't been using it since."

"You mean the jumper?"

"That's right. Maybe it's a clue. I'll tell Grunwald to let the cops know."

After five weeks of intensive labor, the job would be complete with only the barroom work remaining. He entered the room for the first time, needing to take careful measurements and order the correct amount of the flooring Grunwald had selected. The room was deserted except for the bartender, busy cleaning glasses, and two young women in one of the booths, occasionally exchanging words in Spanish.

*The room is too big to do this measuring alone. I'll need help to get the measurements right.* He approached the women, who seemed to be idle except for chatting at leisure. "Perdon, Senoras," he began hesitantly, "necesito … un poco …."

The two women laughed. He retreated a few steps.

"Wait," one of the women said, "We speak English. Habla Englais." She ran a hand through her short, dark hair and smiled at his embarrassment.

He was now aware of her dazzling, dark beauty for the first time. She spoke with only a trace of accent from below the border. "Can we help you with something?"

"Ah, hablas Englais. Bueno. I mean good … good! You speak English. Well, Miss, I just need a hand to hold the end of the tape measure while I measure up the floor."

"I can do that, Senor. My name is Rhonda. This is my sister Rose. We stay here at the hotel. We have seen you coming to work some days. The manager informed us you would be working here too." She slid out from the booth and stood before him. "What will we call you?"'

"It's, ah, I'm, ah, Bowie," he managed after a pause.

*My God—she's the most beautiful woman I've ever seen. The dark eyes. Those full lips.* Suddenly, it seemed it might be too much to ask of her. He stammered, handing her the end of the tape measure. "Can you just ... uh ... hold this tight against the wall while I extend the tape across the room ... please."

Their hands touched, his rough and callused, hers alarmingly soft and warm. "Oh," she said, "strong hands," and repeated to Rose, "manos fuerte, but so rough."

He gazed down at his hands, feeling embarrassed but not insulted or angry as he might have been with others. He looked at her fine hands next to his. "I can find someone else to help."

"No, no, no," she whispered, "I love strong hands." Their eyes met and held for just a moment. "I will help you."

These were feelings he had not experienced before. Confused and timid, he stammered, repeating the simple process of measurement. "We will ... ah ... we will measure the short distance first ... I mean, from here to the bar. You hold the tape ... please ... tight to the wall while I stretch it across the room. Okay?"

She nodded.

"Then I ... we ... will measure the long way. Three times each way. Ready?"

He noted the measurements carefully in his dingy notebook and thanked his beautiful, ad hoc assistant, reluctant to leave the scene.

"Well, goodbye, Rhonda. Adios, Rose. Maybe I can buy you both a drink in return for your help?"

"Thank you, no. It's too early and we will probably be working soon. Bye."

He left, wanting to stay. She watched him go.

## Chapter 21
## Detective Morel

Morgan stood before Denise, seeking approval like a schoolboy on his first day of school. She looked him up and down. Her gaze came to rest on his tie. "I know what to get you for Christmas, but the rest is fine ... Detective Morel." She could not conceal the note of pride in her voice.

Her opinions were still important to him, almost as important as those of his boss, her husband, police captain Douglas MacArthur, who stood beside her at their front door for the early morning inspection. Mac smiled. "Never guess you were a cop."

Morgan shrugged. "You two are great for my ego."

He'd learned a lot from his brief tenure in uniform, and even though he lacked some of the formal training for detectives, he felt quite comfortable in his new skin. Tomorrow morning, he would dig into the most recent reports on the desk in his small office at the station house. The remaining backlog might never be investigated.

"I'm plain-clothes now and not walking a beat," he addressed MacArthur, "do I have plain-clothes transportation?"

"I've renewed our lease for six months for a Chevy Impala with the dealer in Tempe. It will be delivered sometime tomorrow. Hope you like the color. Black."

~~~

Sergeant Aguilar poked his head into Morgan's open office door. "You're here early again. Or didn't you go home last night?"

"I got a couple hours sleep, but I need to wrestle this mess of cases to the ground."

Captain Mac allowed him freedom to manage his workload. For the first few days on the job, he had attempted to triage the backlog of police reports into critical, important, and trivial. He assigned the great majority to the latter category. Now, his typical work day extended to ten or twelve hours dealing with the small minority—in-person investigations of alleged crimes and citizen complaints, interrogations of an occasional perpetrator jailed in the single cell of the station house, stake outs of suspected illicit drug operations—both sales and manufacturing. The crimes were minor—no rapes, murders or kidnappings. Now and then, he was called into court to testify and present the facts of a case. Then, the inevitable hours spent paper shuffling—reading, writing, and filing reports.

But he reserved an hour or two each day to continue the habit, the hobby, of researching unsolved and cold cases he had begun while studying for his degree in civil law. As part of the law enforcement community, he now had access to reports and information beyond what he had as a law student. After all, he would be dealing with criminals and needed to know more about criminal law.

Unidentified corpses, gruesome murder details, unrelated mysteries all held a fascination for him. His memory seemed able to absorb and retain them all. His trained mind often found relationships between seemingly unrelated facts that just might be related after all, like odd pieces of a jigsaw puzzle. He did not consider it part of the job. It was his favorite and only recreation.

He was rarely in his one-bedroom, sparsely furnished apartment except to catch some television news or a few hours of sleep. The twin bed, a necessary purchase, had been bundled with a three-piece kitchenette set from Furnishings Plus for $225, delivery and set up included. The beat-up La-Z-Boy from Denise was the most comfortable chair he'd ever known in spite of the small lumps and slight listing to the left. Often, he would awake in the recliner too late to go to bed but too early to go to the station house. Then, his busy mind would wander. *Will I ever be able to start up the practice I dreamed of? How is Angelica Giles doing, I wonder? Probably a VP in daddy's firm.* Or his thoughts might stray to his years with Mama and Uncle Emile in Wisconsin and to Nancy, his first love. *Is she happy? What if ....*

Sundays were reserved. Work could not infringe on his routine. In the morning, he called Aunt Esther. She seemed happy and occupied, always sharing the latest news of her world. This business opened in town. That one closed. "I'm thinking of opening my own small shop, Morgan! For my paintings and some other local artists and crafters. Maybe a few artsy books. It's just a silly idea, I suppose, but Julia is excited about it too. She likes it here. She might even decide to move in with me."

There might be a late afternoon backyard barbeque with Mac and Denise, but after breakfast of a southwest omelet, coffee, and a quick chat with Mable at the Brew House, he made his way in the black Impala to Phoenix and the Arizona State University law school library to review recent court and IRS decisions and changes in the law. *I need to stay current if my delayed law career ever does get off the ground.*

Meanwhile, his fellow CHPD officers came to regard the young detective with a new respect after he was cited for having assisted solving crimes with neighboring police forces.

"Hey, hotshot, congratulations." Ana pumped his hand. "Those guys in Mesa must have missed a lot of the details you picked up on to crack that case."

"Yeah. They were probably too busy to spend enough time pulling all the facts together. Mesa isn't Cactus Hills where most days we could close the station doors. They have gangs and drugs and population. Two homicides a month. Rapes twice a week. Same for robberies. Too many thefts and burglaries to count. They're always understaffed."

Ana nodded. "I suppose you're right. And now those mall shootings, all in the Mesa area. Three of them, and they don't seem to have a clue except that .270 caliber shell casing they found at one of the scenes. Maybe you can help them with that too."

Mac stepped up and handed him a new Mesa PD report. "Well, you might be able to help with their problems again. I agreed with their request for you to handle the investigation of an apparent suicide at the TruFont Hotel. From what I hear, it's no Hilton. But don't forget, we need you here. You don't need to accept the assignment."

It didn't take long to decide. "I'm in. Any chance it wasn't suicide?"

"That is what the ME report says, but that will be for you to decide if you uncover new evidence, detective."

Morgan made the TruFont his last call on a day that included reports on an overnight break-in and theft of computers and printers at Technology Supply and a domestic disturbance where the irate wife's three shots from a BB-gun had wounded the accused husband's dignity but did no other observable damage. Then there was the persisting complaint on Delphi Street that the neighbor's dog had again done her duty on old Mrs. Albertus's carefully raked and spotlessly maintained front yard.

He had undertaken this latter matter at Harvey's urgent plea after his frustrated former beat-cop partner had failed to resolve the recurrent dispute. It had been a near-daily occurrence for the previous six months. "Morgan, I've seen you settle domestic tangles with your magic talent to bring peace out of chaos. I challenge you with this one."

He discovered Mrs. Albertus had not actually met her new neighbor. "No, and I don't ever want to meet him and his damned," she blushed with shame and anger, "perpetually pooping dog."

After thirty minutes of threats, cajoling, negotiations, and shameless flattery, he brought the unwilling neighbors together for a discussion, their first face-to-face meeting.

Another thirty minutes later, after irate threats of lawsuits and physical violence abated, the retired school teacher and the part-time preacher were smiling over afternoon tea in Mrs. Albertus's quaint living room, happy to have made each other's lonely acquaintances and, at last, pledged to resolve the continuously recurrent and gut-wrenching issue of errant dog poop.

The TruFont desk clerk confirmed what the police report had shown. The single woman, age estimated around 50, had checked in at 10PM without luggage other than a large shoulder bag. At midnight, her body had crashed onto the parking lot pavement three floors below. An empty fifth of Jameson's was later recovered in the room. The purse contained no identification. The only conclusion Morgan could make now was her good taste in liquor.

Jo-Jo, the bartender, did not recall seeing the woman in the bar. "It was a slow night." He motioned toward the booth across the room where two young women sat chatting. "Maybe them two in the booth might know something. They're almost always here. They live here in the hotel."

Morgan glanced at his watch. Almost seven. He hadn't had lunch, and his stomach was growling. Still, he couldn't leave without speaking with possible witnesses.

"I'm Detective Morel with the Cactus Hills Police."

*Why are these two beauties sitting around in a two-bit hotel bar?*

The two women exchanged worried glances.

"Jo-Jo told me you are often here. I wonder if either of you ladies know anything about the suicide that happened here last week? Were you here when it happened?"

"Yes, sir. But we know nothing." Two sets of dark eyes remained carefully diverted from meeting his questioning gaze.

"Well, do you remember seeing anyone strange in the hotel that night?

"No, sir. No strangers."

"Jo-Jo mentioned you live here. Could I please have your names in case I need to contact you again about this?"

They exchanged furtive glances again. *What are they so worried about?*

"We know nothing, sir. Can we leave now?"

"Just give me your names, if you don't mind. You're in no trouble. It might help me."

He carefully scratched their names in his notebook. Rhonda and Rose Rogers.

"Thank you then, ladies." He laid his card on the booth table. "Please call if anything new comes to mind. I appreciate speaking with you both. Have a good evening."

In the morning, he submitted his brief report to the Mesa PD. No evidence to suggest that this was not suicide. I was not able to discover anything more of the victim's identity. Assignment complete.

But his meeting with the two reluctant witnesses was never far from his mind. For the following week, he considered various reasons why he might return to the TruFont hotel and how he could manage to meet again with the beautiful Rogers sisters.

Then Grunwald called him. "With all the renovation work going on here, I forgot to tell you and the Mesa Police something. I just now remembered. Might not be important, but we found some keys in the room the suicide victim used. Do you want to see them?"

## Chapter 22
## Mamas' Boys

When Morgan arrived at the hotel late that afternoon, Bowie and Grunwald stood eyeing the new barroom floor installation. "Looks great, even better than expected," the manager said, "and all the work completed on schedule. Come to my office. I'll cut you a check, including the $500 bonus."

Bowie nodded. "Yeah, thanks. I like it, too." He looked across the room to where the Rogers sisters sat chatting. "I see my assistant and her friend are here."

As he and the happy hotel manager turned to leave the room, they encountered Morgan entering. "Hello, Mr. Grunwald. The clerk told me where to find you. I'm here for those keys you called me about."

"Yes, they're in my office. We were just heading that way. Detective Morel, this is Bowie Masters, the genius who installed this beautiful new flooring. And by the way, he also found the keys while working in room 303. Bowie, this is Detective Morel. He's been looking into that woman's suicide."

The men nodded and silently shook hands, then followed the manager to his office.

Grunwald searched the litter on his desk to find the hotel checkbook. "Let me write out this check for Masters so he can be on his way if you don't mind waiting a few moments, Detective."

"Not a problem." Morgan turned to Bowie. "Can you tell me anything about finding the keys?"

"Nothing much to tell. They must have been under the bed. I had to move it to make room to work. It's a small room. Keys were there on the floor. Figured someone lost them, so I turned them over to the clerk, but apparently, no one ever claimed them. Are they important?"

"Might be. Maybe connect us to a car ... the victim's car if they're her keys. That would help ID her. I'll run the numbers through the database as soon as I return to the station."

Grunwald handed Bowie a check and the set of car keys to Morgan. "Now, gentlemen, if you will please excuse me, the clerk seems to be having a problem." He showed them out of his office and made his way to the front desk, one more problem to solve in his busy life.

Bowie said, "Think I'll take one more look at my handiwork in the barroom. Maybe my beautiful assistant will be there for me to thank again. Good luck with your case."

Morgan said, "I'll join you. I'm off duty now. Can I buy you a drink?" Maybe he would conjure up a reason for seeing the Rogers sisters again, though, at the moment, he had no pretext for doing so, only hope and desire.

After years of studiously avoiding any contact with the law, Bowie found himself walking down the hallway lined with concession and soft drink machines, side by side with a cop, a detective. It was almost ten years since Big John and Billy the Kid. No way he could be connected now with either of them. He'd almost forgotten them himself. He was reputable now, a homeowner, a tax-paying citizen. "Okay. Maybe just one if Jo-Jo has a cold beer."

They entered the wide doorway labeled Fiesta Room with a small sign noting *Ice Here.* Disappointment rose in Morgan's eyes as he scanned the barroom. The booth was empty.

He ordered drinks. "A cold beer for my friend Mr. Masters ... Bowie, right? Make mine a rum and coke. Go easy on the rum." Since his overindulgence in Sturgis with Son of Satan, he almost always abstained from liquor except for a rare glass of wine with Douglas and Denise MacArthur.

He pointed to the vacant booth. "Weren't the Rogers sisters just here? Do you know where they went, Jo-Jo? I'd hoped to speak with them again."

"I think they went out for a walk. Get a little fresh air. It's a few degrees cooler now before nightfall. The boss will want them back soon, in case any lonely customers show up tonight." He went to get a Dos Equis and mix a rum and coke. He could handle a short shot of rum. He would use the phony jigger he always used for the sisters' drinks.

Bowie shot a glance in Morgan's direction. "Were you asking about Rhonda and Rose? I didn't know they were sisters ... suppose I should have, they look almost identical. How do you happen to know them?"

"I spoke with them briefly about the suicide case. I got the definite impression they were not pleased to talk with me. Hoped I might be able to change that if we ever met again."

After three rounds of drinks, Rhonda and Rose had not yet returned. Their resolve possibly fortified by alcohol, both Bowie and Morgan now seemed quite determined to remain until the sisters returned. They lapsed into casual conversation.

Bowie sipped his beer, searching for something to say. "What do you think of the D-backs new manager?"

"I'm not really a baseball fan, but it did cause a splash in the papers and on television. At least it displaced Obama and the economy for a while. Are you a fan?"

"You mean of Obama or the Diamond Backs?"

Morgan laughed. "Baseball."

"Never been to Chase Field for a game. I listen to them on the radio sometimes while I work. Helps pass the time."

The detective's instinct to search for detail, even in trivia, kicked in. "What exactly is work?"

Bowie replied easily. "I'm Masters of Masters Construction. Been handling small, odd jobs all around the Mesa area where I have a home. My partner and I used to build houses, but this TruFont work is the first big job I've had since the housing bust. How about you? What kind of cop are you?"

Morgan's cell phone chirped. He looked at it and hit mute.

Bowie asked, "Aren't you going to answer? Maybe official business? Don't mind me."

Morgan slipped the phone into his pocket. "That was Mama. I didn't call her at the usual time. I suppose she's worried. I'll call her later."

"You can still talk with your mama?"

"Every week for the past year since I've been away from her. She's really my aunt, but I call her Mama. My real mama died years ago. My dad too."

"I lost my mama and daddy when I was real young too. But ...." Bowie stopped speaking. He turned to Jo-Jo. "This one's gone flat. Another round."

Morgan put up a hand. "Not for me, thanks, but you go ahead." He went on to explain his fortuitous contact with Uncle Emile and Aunt Esther after his parents died and how his uncle financed his law school education after he went to live with them when he was seventeen.

Bowie said. "At least you know they're dead, and now you have a home with someone who cares for you." He took a deep swallow from the bottle Jo-Jo handed him. He belched loudly and muttered to himself, "Could my mama still be alive somewhere?" He looked at Morgan, "It's been almost twenty years since she ran off. I don't know if my mama is alive or dead ... but she's dead to me, and I know I'm dead to her."

Morgan watched the stoic mask of his companion slowly dissolve into a look of helpless sadness, tears gathering in his eyes, then quickly recover to hide the momentary weakness.

Bowie swept his hands in an *I-don't-know* gesture, upsetting the half-full beer bottle and sending a sea of foam down the bar. "Oh, goddamnit!"

"I'll get it," Jo-Jo said, "make that one on the house."

Morgan said, "Maybe it's time to leave. We should talk again sometime. I'd like to get to know you better, get to know more about your life."

Jo-Jo suggested, "You could wait for Rhonda and Rose over there in their booth. Pretty sure they'll be returning soon."

"Okay, bring us another round then."

As they sat waiting in the booth, Bowie remained silent, intent on his beer bottle, avoiding eye contact with Morgan. Morgan attempted to lead a conversation, trying to discover more of what lay behind his friend's reticence to openly share his feelings, the mental and emotional tug of war he had witnessed. Bowie listened intently to the story of Morgan's motorcycle trip to Sturgis and camping out at Buffalo Chip, the tale sparking his own recollections. "So, you were a tent camper too? I camped out in the Coconino Forest once. I caught fish and small game to cook for dinner. It was great. I was alone until …." He stopped abruptly again. Morgan wondered *and what's the rest of the story?*

Morgan's interest in Bowie had started simply and routinely as habitual fact-gathering—a cop thing. Peering into those steel-gray eyes, he was challenged to know more, to learn more of the enigmatic man who seemed so vulnerable and yet so distant. He knew that even while uncovering nuances of his character, he had not penetrated Bowie's complex defenses. The man seemed to have secrets. Deep secrets. His empathy for his fellow humans combined with his affinity for solving mysteries. He wanted, he needed to understand their origins.

While they sat quietly together, he thought of those who he had been closest to since his mother and father died without warning. There were his dear aunts and uncle, of course, close family. But what of his friends? It seemed he had always been too busy to form lasting friendships. Nancy Feldstein, his teen love, his first sex. Angelica's relationship was far more intellectual than physical, fellow law students. He loved Denise as the sister he didn't have. Three women—his closest friends. He had never had a brother to share his life. Mac, his mentor, was perhaps as close as he'd ever come to having a close male friend.

Rhonda Rogers, fresh from an evening stroll, entered the Fiesta Bar with her sister at her side. "Look, there is someone in our booth." As they walked across the shiny new flooring, she recognized both intruders. "Halo Mister Measuring Man. Are you happy with your new floor? Here comes Rose, too." She placed her hand on Bowie's bare arm. "Do you want to buy us both a nice drink now and invite us to sit in the booth?" She turned to her sister. "And look, Rose, it is Detective Morel, too. Do you think we are in trouble?"

# Chapter 23
# Maria & Mateo

Rose's letters to her home in Mexico always began with questions. How are you and Papi? How is our little home in little Islita? What are my young brothers and sisters doing? Then she assured her mother she and her twin sister were healthy and prosperous, often enclosing some American dollars as proof, even if it meant she and Rhonda did not eat that day. She told of how they prayed at the shrine early every morning, knowing their parents would be pleased.

> It opens at 6 AM, and almost no one is ever there, not even the priest. Then we might sit in the park for a while Sometimes, there are children playing, and we think of home and our young brothers and sisters. Sometimes, in winter, there are ducks in the little lake. After a while, we go to work all day.

Often in the margin or on a separate sheet, she penciled a sketch of a scene from the streets around the hotel or the park—a tiny squirrel with paws in the air, a phoebe or crested titmouse perched on a branch, or an inverted nuthatch. Once, she included a profile sketch of Jo-Jo, *our friend from the hotel where we live.* Another time, a sketch of her sister asleep in a chair.

Maria replied, sending her letter to the P.O. Box return address.

Your letter and little drawings are so beautiful. We have saved them all in a book. The little birds remind me and Papi of you and Vanessa. Yes, I know she is Rhonda now.

The twins, Carlos and Carlita, are graduating from high school. They will be leaving our little casa soon. Carlos took some vocational classes and wants to be an automobile mechanic or maybe work at a GM plant and earn lots of money. But so far away, almost 5000 kilometers. When will we see him again? Carlita has perfect grades. She wants to attend university. Maybe she can get a scholarship. But what do you know of Ernesto? We have no word from him all these years since he left with you for America.

Papi's garden is bigger now, and we sell all he grows. But gracias for all the money. I enclose all our love. Mama.

 Rose's reply included two one hundred-dollar bills. She explained that she and Rhonda had earned some extra money posing for an art class at the Mesa Arts Center.

I showed the instructor some of my little sketches too. She liked them. My faces especially. She said I maybe could be a sidewalk portrait artist.

 She did not note that the art class was *The Human Figure* and that they posed nude.

We have not seen Ernesto since he brought us here. What he does is dangerous. Maybe he is hiding.

Maria and Mateo Rodriguez missed all of their children who had fledged their nest. Their four youngest would soon finish elementary school, then high school too. Soon, their nest would be empty. They were grateful to still see Carlita, the first to seek higher education, twice a year. They hoped Carlos would come soon to tell them of his work. Maybe he would be driving a big new Chevy Silverado or GMC Sierra when he got some vacation time. But would they ever see Vanessa and Violetta again? With their new names and new lives, they lived only a few hundred miles away across the border, closer than some of their other children. Could they ever return to Mexico to visit them, to be held and adored?

Maria was excited to show her husband Rose's most recent letter. "Mateo, look what Violetta has sent this time."

"Money again? You must tell her they must save their money, not to send it always home."

"No. Better than money. Come and look. Photographs. Our two daughters smiling. But they look so thin. If only I could fix them some good home-cooked meals … my beef empanadas and corn from your garden or chilaquiles and cake with cream and strawberries."

Mateo said. "They look strong enough, and they are smiling. They must be happy. Who are the strange men? They are not Mexican."

Maria read.

> We have found new friends in America—hombres Americanos. Really, they found us at the hotel not long ago. Now they come to see us many days. Sometimes both come and sometimes one or the other. The one with the long hair and serious face is called Bowie.

*He came to the hotel to fix things. He asked Rhonda (Vanessa) to help him one day. She likes him. He is kind to her and sometimes gives her little gifts—flowers or candy. He smiles when he sees her, but he is very quiet and always seems sad.*

*The other man, the one wearing the suit and necktie, is called Morgan. He is very smart. He makes us laugh with funny stories, even Bowie. I like him very much, but I am afraid to love him. He is a lawman who came to the hotel one day to ask us questions. He came back again later and asked if he could take me and Rhonda to a new TexMex restaurant. We said okay, but we would have liked the Thai place better. He gave cameras to Rhonda and me when he learned it was our birthday, so now you have photographs. Can you believe we are 25?*

Maria sighed. "Of course, we know it was your birthdays last month. Yes, 25, our first-born twins." She wiped away a tear and continued to read the next page of Rose's letter.

*Bowie and Morgan are good friends. Bowie owns a big house outside the city with some land. We visit there sometimes—all of us together, after Rhonda and I have gone to the early mass on Sunday. He is thinking of keeping horses on his land. He is building a big barn all by himself—he is a very good builder. He has a housekeeper who lives in the house. She fixes us dinner sometimes—a big meal with meat and vegetables—but she is old* and not always feeling well. Then Bowie makes tacos or hamburgers, and we drink beer, but not Morgan.

We never visit Morgan's home. He says it is too small for all of us. He invited us to visit his friends named, MacArthur. Bowie said Rhonda and I should go, but he refused because Mr. MacArthur is a police captain.

Maria said to Mateo, "So our daughters have men friends. I never had a good talk with them about men. Maybe I should write and warn them now."

Mateo frowned. "Warn them? Are all of us so bad you must warn them? Are you not happy with me after all these years?"

"But you are the exception, Mateo, my love. Not every woman can be as lucky as I was." She turned to her husband and, with a hand on each cheek, kissed him gently on the lips.

## Chapter 24
## Friends & Lovers

Rhonda called Bowie's cell phone. "Rose and I will be busy today. You and Morgan must not come to see us at the hotel."

"Okay, Rhonda. Are you and Rose okay?"

"Just promise me you won't come today."

"Whatever you say then. We'll miss you."

Morgan was chatting with Aunt Esther just as Bowie's text message came in on his iPhone.

"How long will you stay in Arizona, Morgan? Your motorcycle ride to take a little break seems to have become permanent. When will I see you again?"

"I don't know, Mama. I've heard nothing from the BBE since I left Wisconsin more than a year ago. Meanwhile, life goes on."

With an audible sigh, "Tell me you're happy and well, at least."

"I'm fine. Are you okay? You sound well. How is Aunt Julia?"

"Well, I'm painting again … a little. Julia has taken over most of the cooking and chores while I take my paints and easel out and try to capture the beauty of the countryside. Says she loves the chickens. Says they have more personality than lobsters." Mama laughed.

"She's a fair cook, and I'm happy to have a change of menu. I would miss her badly if she left now."

"Please give her my love. I hope to see her before she leaves."

His phone beeped a text. *From Bowie, wonder what he needs.*

"I'll have to go now, Mama—another call. Talk with you soon. Love you. Bye."

He hit the red "end" button and read the text message.

> Rhonda warned me we must not come to the hotel today. You should come to my place. I got an idea for something we can do without them for a change.

Morgan was happy to take the Harley out for a ride. Bowie was outside working on the new horse barn when he roared up the unpaved driveway. He watched his friend dismounting from the extension ladder to stand and appraise his work. "Roof is finished. Now for some red paint … or dark stain or whitewash. What do you think?"

"Red."

Bowie unbuckled his tool belt and slung it on his shoulder. "I'll be looking for something to fill the stalls soon … at least two good riding horses. Would like to get four and all the gear, so we could all ride together. Two is all I can afford now … can't spend more than six or seven thousand. I haven't been on horseback since the rodeo and the Double-U ranch. Do you ride?"

Morgan laughed. "I have never been up on a horse. The bike is plenty ride for me. Pretty sure Rose and Rhonda haven't ever been on a horse's back either.

Why did Rhonda say we couldn't come to the hotel today?"

Bowie collapsed the ladder. "Wouldn't say. Must have extra work or something."

Morgan's laugh ended, replaced by an angry scowl. "They aren't supposed to work today. Extra work? What would they be doing?" he asked, even though he knew the answer.

"Like I said, all she said was not to come. But relax, I have plans for us."

Not much interested, Morgan kicked the driveway gravel and grumbled, "Fine, let's have it … your plan." His thoughts were still on the TruFont hotel.

"Thought it would be a good day for some shooting … target practice. Then I checked my Winchester. Funny thing, it had been fired sometime, but I don't remember firing it since Lee Roy and I used it. I always clean it after a shoot. A gift from a friend, years ago. It deserves good care."

They drove in Bowie's truck to the quarry. Morgan remained quiet—moody, and distracted.

At the deserted quarry, Bowie loaded five rounds into the rifle. "I suppose they taught you something about shooting in cop school?"

"Some small arms instruction." He thought of Mac's hurried instructions on the firing range to push him through police training. "More gun safety and handling than target practice. Tasers and nightsticks too. But I can shoot."

Bowie nodded and said, "It's almost 300 yards to the other side. See that shiny quartz sticking out directly across? Watch and learn."

The sparking quartz target disappeared as all five rounds bore into it, scattering fragments and leaving a small dent in the quarry wall.

Morgan's interest perked up. "Pretty impressive shooting, Bowie. Where did you learn?"

"Mostly practicing right here with Lee Roy, but I earned a sharpshooter medal in the Marines boot camp."

"You never mentioned you were in the Marines." Morgan thought, *one of his many secrets?* "Where did you train?"

"California. But I didn't stay in the corps." He handed Morgan five rounds. "Here, you load."

The acrid smell of gun smoke fouled his nostrils and watered his eyes. He wiped a sweaty sleeve across his face, took the shells and loaded. "These are .270 caliber, aren't they? I think that's the same as they found at one of the recent mall shootings. Not real common. Have you read about those shootings? Single victims, all women."

"Guess I missed that. I don't get the paper."

Morgan's thoughts were still on the TruFont hotel. He located a target on the far quarry wall. He squeezed and squeezed the trigger. *Goddamnit, goddamnit, goddamnit, goddamnit, GOD DAMN IT!* He fired as fast as he could work the bolt, not seeing where any of the rounds hit.

~~~

Denise stuck out her lower lip in a coy, exaggerated little pout "This is at least four or five Sundays running that you have rejected my invitation for dinner. I know you're always hungry, so what's going on? Is Mac working you too hard? Are you upset with me

… with us, or are we just passé?" She batted her eyes in mock distress.

"Afraid I'll have to run again. I just stopped by to see how you and the kids are, the twins, and the new baby. What's her name?"

"We call her Dumpling, but she doesn't have a name yet. Almost a year old."

"Well, nothing is up, and you know I love you and miss seeing you. Of course, I see Mac at the station house all the time, but we don't talk personal stuff. I've been busy, pure and simple."

This was the truth, though not the whole truth. Detective Morel's official assignments were more than enough to keep him busy, but he wouldn't give up aiding neighboring forces' investigations in addition. This was not entirely altruistic—it added immensely to his practical experience and understanding of policing, investigation, and the law, far beyond what he would ever learn at the CHPD. Fortunately, once Captain Mac recommended him, no one asked about his investigative credentials.

Then there was reading the Police Chief Magazine he appropriated from Mac's desk and pouring over the American Bar Association online journal and weekly newsletters, the Wall Street Journal and Financial Advisor Monthly. And he never failed to take time for his hobby of researching unsolved crimes that had begun in law school, even if for just a few hours each week. Now, with limited time, he had narrowed his search to Arizona crimes within the last fifteen to twenty years.

Denise looked him in the eye. "There is a woman, isn't there."

"Look, Denise, we can talk about this later sometime, but I really have to go now."

She gave him a derisive, hurt look and a quick hug. "Bye, then."

Morgan drove the police car to pick up Rhonda and Rose at the hotel, thinking. *Seems as if pure chance has ruled my life until now. But for you two taking a long evening stroll, I might never have become more than slightly acquainted with Bowie Masters. And, how different would my life have been had I not wandered into Sturgis and, because of a hangover, met Denise MacArthur? Even finding Mama's and Uncle Emile's phone number was pure luck. What would I have done without them to love and guide me? But Rose ... can I choose to love you now?*

He was quite sure Bowie wanted to be his friend too, that he needed a close friend. He had made efforts to further the relationship, still superficial perhaps. But, his could-be friend remained an enigma and carefully guarded. What secrets was he guarding? Why was he not willing to fully trust him? Most people did. It was probably his best asset.

He pulled into the hotel parking lot. Almost noon. Rhonda and Rose waited outside. The three of them headed out to Bowie's house outside of town for lunch and a light dinner. After lunch prepared by Old Josephina, the four friends might gather in the comfortable living room, relaxed and happy to be together, sharing bits of their past lives and future hopes in casual conversation. Bowie rarely added to those exchanges. He seemed more comfortable watching a sports event, concert, or movie on his big 42-inch flat screen television. After dinner, typically soup and salad or lunch leftovers, the conversation continued with a glass of wine for Morgan and the sisters and a beer for Bowie.

Rhonda paced around the living room, admiring the furnishings. "You have such good taste, Bowie. Nothing matches, but it all fits together ... a little bit like the four of us, yes?"

"It's all Lee Roy's stuff. I kept it all."

Rhonda came to a collection of CDs. "This is great, must be hundreds of discs. Is it Lee Roy's too?"

"For sure."

"Oh, I love these oldies ... 40s, 50s, and 60s. Look, Rose," as she scanned labels, "the Beatles, Ella, Patsy Cline, Dean Martin, Sinatra ... a little of everything."

She picked out a country-western album. "May I play this, Bowie?"

"Your pleasure is my pleasure?"

Patsy Cline's voice floated across the room while the foursome listened silently—*Sweet Dreams, Crazy, I Fall to Pieces.*

"Dance with me, Bowie," she pleaded. She pulled him to his feet and close to her. They swayed, slow and easy to the rhythm of the music. She took his hand to lead him out of the room—to be alone. "Let's explore." Bowie did not resist.

Rose and Morgan sat watching each other from separate stuffed chairs. Rose came to her feet to peruse the CD collection. She sipped the last of her glass of Chianti. "Oh, here's one."

She ejected the Patsy Cline disc and inserted one labeled *Exotic Guitar* into the Bose player.

Kicking off her sandals, she swayed to the slow, steady rhythm. She padded barefoot in a wide circle around the room and stopped in front of Morgan. She moved her arms slowly, extending them wide, side to side, while her hips moved to the hypnotic beat and melody of the lone guitar. Her fingers fluttered as she raised her slender arms above her head while she turned, gyrating slowly in a small circle. Her shear muslin shift clung to her body, revealing luscious curves, hips, and breasts. Her bare feet marked the driving beat on the wooden floor. She tossed her head side to side, mesmerized and excited.

The guitar sang a last shrill note. The music stopped. She dropped the flimsy shift from her shoulders, then to the floor. She stood naked before Morgan. Then she was on him, straddling his legs with hers, hard nipples brushing his face. Her lips on his, her tongue searching, her hand on the increasing bulge, his fly opened.

Then he was in her. Oh, God, it had been so long, so long. Her movements held him, held him, not for long. He exploded, his pent emotions released all at once.

Rose stepped back to the floor and pulled on her dress and sandals. Rhonda and Bowie strolled back into the room, hand in hand, smiling. "So, how are you two getting along?" Rhonda inquired.

Morgan stammered, "I suppose it's time for us to go, but there is a thing I want to discuss, a thing that has been long on my mind." Rose's scent was still in his nostrils, the image of her naked body still in his harassed mind. "Have you girls tried to find work other than the hotel?"

Rose answered, "The hotel work is easy. Working together, we always finish cleaning by noon. Then we can shower and change clothes. Most afternoons, we wait in the barroom to talk or play chess or write a letter home. Whatever. Sometimes we chat with customers, men customers as Mr. Grunwald likes us to do, men with time on their hands and money to spend."

Listening to her, Morgan's usual calm equanimity evaporated word by word. "Rose, I don't want you entertaining the male customers anymore! Rhonda too!"

"But we must work, Morgan. We must eat. We must live."

"Find other work!" His rage was building, almost out of control.

Rose confirmed what Morgan suspected. "We tried at first. We don't have documents. We can't get green cards. No one will hire us!"

The woman he wanted to love was an illegal working as a prostitute in a shabby hotel.

"There must be something else for you both. Bowie, do you want Rhonda working at the hotel?"

Bowie rubbed both temples with the heels of his palms. "Why are you bringing this up now? We get along fine, don't we, the four or us? I suppose they have to do what they have to do."

Morgan was on his feet. "Goddamnit, Bowie, is that the best you have? I know how you feel about Rhonda. How can you tolerate it?"

Rhonda's eyes brimmed with tears—tears of fright, tears of shame. "I'm sorry, Bowie. I'm sorry, Morgan," she sobbed.

"Fuck this!" Morgan screamed, "You take the whores back to where they belong. I'm leaving." He strode to the door and did not look back. The door slamming shook the room.

Bowie and the Rogers sisters did not see him again for three weeks.

~~~

Morgan filled his days and nights with work and study, attempting to ignore the images of Rose Rogers that intruded into his thoughts. He drew a sharp intake of air into his lungs. He paused whatever he was attempting to accomplish, distracted, dejected and angry. He wanted to be with her. He was miserable without her. But what could he do?

Sitting in the Fiesta Room booth, Rose, Rhonda, and Bowie watched Morgan trudge into the barroom. Jo-Jo looked up. "Hey, Morgan, long time no see."

"Hi, Jo-Jo. Sorry, I've been real busy." He crossed the floor and stood next to the booth. Looking at Rose, he asked, "Is it okay if I join you?"

Bowie answered, "Have you cooled off enough yet?"

Morgan ignored him. "Please, Rose. Please, Rhonda. I need to talk with the three of you."

Rose smiled. "You know you are welcome!" Color rose to her cheeks. "Sit here next to me."

Morgan looked at each of them, one by one. "I have a plan."

Bowie and the two women listened while he explained his ideas. Bowie has a big house with several vacant rooms. His old housekeeper can barely walk—much less care for the house properly. The women could leave the hotel to live in Bowie's rooms and take over the housekeeping, maybe cooking. If they needed money, Morgan would get it for them somehow.

"I know it's shaky, but it's all I have. We must do something. It's a start. We can work it out. Okay?"

Rose hugged her sister. Could this be the change they prayed for every day? Then, she reached out to take Morgan's two hands in hers. They regarded each other through tear-filled, hopeful eyes.

Bowie grinned. "Shit yeah. It's fine with me."

Maybe this shift would change his life, too. Maybe with close friends around him, the Monster would leave him now.

## Chapter 25
## Coconspirators

Big John couldn't help feeling hostile and low-down. He winced. His old wounds were acting up, jabs of sharp, unexpected pain. And his once-in-a-while, long-time girlfriend, Maria, had emphatically dumped him last month. "You no fun. I don wan see you no more!"

Maybe he had assumed too much. She had always been there in the past, the only simpatico human contact he'd had for years. She had even come to visit during his long hospital convalescence when no one else expected him to live. Now, she was gone.

His rig was at Universal Truck and Trailer Services for long overdue maintenance—tires, transmission, electrical systems, diesel engine—the works. *That'll cost, and it won't be ready until tomorrow. Hope I can contract a load then to somewhere, anywhere.*

In late morning, he'd checked into the TruFont, Royal Treatment at Budget Prices, and sprawled fully clothed on the hotel bed to catch up on his sleep. The afternoon sun through the unshaded window woke him. *Jeez, what time is it? I need some food or a drink or a fix.*

He pulled on his eye patch and took the stairs down to the lobby desk when the elevator failed to respond to his repeated jabbing of the call button. "You serve food here?"

"Might find a little something in the Fiesta Room bar, just down the hall at the end."

"Thanks."

The bar room was sparsely occupied. Two women occupied a booth, hookers, he guessed, waiting for some action of the evening and the burly barkeep.

"Shot of Cuervo. Make it a double … and a Dos Equis."

"Coming right up."

"Desk clerk said I could find something to eat here too."

"Just burgers and tacos today. They're frozen. I nuke 'em up. Not as bad as it sounds."

"Two burgers, then, I'm starved."

"I can give you fries too, or refried beans."

"Okay. Fries. You got a name?"

"Yes, Sir, they call me Jo-Jo."

Big John sipped the warm tequila. Tension in his neck and shoulders eased a little.

Two men entered the bar room from a rear door he hadn't noticed before. One wore a suit and tie, even in the afternoon heat. The hotel AC helped some, but not much. The other man was dressed in jeans, a ragged work shirt, dirty boots, and a sweat-stained baseball cap. Both took a seat in the booth with the two dark-haired women. *Maybe not hookers after all, or maybe their johns just showed up.*

His burgers and fries arrived, steaming hot. Jo-Jo put up plates of salsa and stuffed jalapenos. "Extras are on the house for hotel guests. You're staying here, right?"

"Just tonight until my rig is ready."

"Oh, you're a driver. That eyepatch give you any problems on the road?"

Big John savored a sip of the cold beer for a moment before answering. "Got used to it years ago. Hardly notice it except for tight parking situations. Got a special license to drive one-eyed." He laughed and reached for the quarter-pounder.

Jo-Jo wiped the bar with a well-used rag. "Cool. Let me know if you need anything else."

Big John dug into his food order, his first nourishment since a microwave breakfast burrito at the truck stop. Finished, he motioned Jo-Jo to come closer. He whispered, "How's chances for a little fix around here, some Speed, you know, No Doze."

Jo-Jo glanced cautiously around the near-vacant room and up and down the vacant bar.

"See the guy over there in the booth? Not the suit. The other one."

Big John pivoted to catch a glimpse of the back of the grimy baseball cap. "Yeah. He doesn't look too reliable. I want clean stuff, fine stuff, something I can snort to gear up."

"Well," Jo-Jo hesitated, "He doesn't deal, but I think he was a user … and he has a lot of contacts. He might know someone who could help you out. Just tell him Jo-Jo sent you."

"Is he a regular? He looks real cozy with the other three."

"He actually did a lot of renovation work here at the hotel. Don't recall how the four of them got acquainted. They hung out here every day for a while, then not. Today is the first I've seen them all together again. They're acting thick as thieves now. Up to something, I'm guessing."

Big John downed the last of his beer and stepped away from the bar stool. He glanced around the room. Still no other customers. He headed toward the booth where the two men and two women chatted, four heads close together as if plotting insurrection. He angled to get a better look at the alleged supplier contact, eyes trained on the men.

*Both about the same age. Could the suit be a cop? Sure has that look. Maybe the barkeep gave me a bum steer.* He sized up the other man and stopped in his tracks. *I know that face!*

The face was years older now than when he had seen it last. Shoulder-length hair replaced the crew cut, but it was a face he would never forget. Ten feet from the booth, the rage that had lived within him for a decade rose instantly. His heart pounded. His teeth clenched. His hands tightened into massive, hard fists. *Wait. Wait, I need to figure how to end this at last.* Big John wheeled, left the bar, and returned to his room to plot his revenge.

# Chapter 26
# Unwelcome Suspicions

Morgan slipped out of the booth and walked up to the empty bar. It would not be empty later once the regulars and a few hotel guests started filtering in. "Pitcher of the usual Jo-Jo and two glasses. Margs on the rocks for the women. It's a sort of celebration, so use the real stuff."

Jo-Jo filled two glasses with ice, commercial margarita mix, and a shot of cheap, house tequila. He drew the draft slowly, allowing the foam to settle. Morgan delivered the margaritas to the booth and returned to the bar. "Put it on my tab, as usual. I'll be back to settle up tomorrow morning. Uh … your only customer … the pirate guy with the patch … left in a hurry. Looked like he might be coming to talk to us."

"Yeah. Go figure. Said he was looking for some meth. I sent him over to see Bowie. Thought he might have a contact even though I know he's not using any more. The guy started over there, then froze like he'd seen a ghost. Shot outa here without settling his tab. They'll catch that when he checks out tomorrow."

"So, he won't be back in here?"

"Don't think so. And I'm sorry about the Crank. I know that's a touchy area with you."

"Forget it, Jo-Jo, but I'd rather not be around when that sort of thing is going on."

He brought the pitcher and two empty glasses to the booth. "Cold beer here!"

They had been kicking around his idea about leaving the hotel to live with Bowie. Or what about crossing the border back into Mexico and not returning? He had to admit the idea probably had some appeal for the women, but it would be highly unlikely that he would ever see Rose again, and Bowie would not see Rhonda. No, thank God, they would go with his plan for a start, and the start would be tomorrow when the sisters gave notice to Grunwald they were moving out. Okay, case closed, let's celebrate.

His mind turned to the other things, matters that had been troubling him, matters concerning his enigmatic friend, Bowie Masters. He had put his recent suspicions aside—farfetched—but the curious mind of the detective would not be silent. He had observed his friend's several extreme sides. He'd seen the irate, out-of-control, vicious slap when Rhonda called him Bows, "I told you never to call me that," and the rapid melting into gentle compassion and contrition. "I'm so sorry, Babe, please forgive me," and the two sharing their tears.

He knew the bright, inquisitive mind that never read a book but could build a house. He loved the spontaneous laughter, the goodwill, the charm. He'd seen Bowie with children—gentle pats on the head, his generous smiles when doling out small candies he always kept in his pockets for no other purpose.

Most of all, he was aware of the black moods that gripped his friend, unexpectedly and unexplained, when no one and nothing could touch him, as if suddenly demon-possessed, unable to control his own actions, wracked with unbearable headaches and forgetfulness.

What of those shreds of evidence that had been haunting him lately? He couldn't call it evidence really, but rather vague clues, unwelcome suspicions, pieces of a complex, incomplete jigsaw puzzle, most of the pieces missing.

There was little beyond his doubts and intuitions to connect his friend to several crimes he'd come upon in the cold case files, details retained somewhere in his detective brain. Bowie would have been just a teenage kid at the time. The only unlikely clues a Marine combat knife and service automatic pistol, the stolen property reported by a California training base—a 9mm Beretta automatic along with a combat knife. Then Bowie had mentioned his Marine Corps training at the recruit center in California whose quartermaster had reported the items missing. *Probably pure coincidence.*

The knife was reported recovered, nothing worth noting except it was still in the eye of a semi-driver who had been viciously attacked and left for dead. Oddly too, the Beretta was later recovered in a dry stream bed not far from where the trucker attack had occurred, along with the discovery of a teenage boy's badly beaten body in the Coconino Forest. *Isn't that where Bowie had described a brief, joyful camping trip at about that time?*

And the recent Mesa shopping mall shootings. That was really farfetched. Yes, Bowie lived in the vicinity. So did millions of others. But millions of others did not own a vintage rifle of the same rare caliber as the round that killed the victims. *What motivation would he have had?*

No, these suspicions didn't add up to anything sinister about Bowie. Still, he knew he would be compelled to investigate further. He would gently query his friend further about his Marine Corps and camping experiences. And the mall shootings. Tomorrow.

Tomorrow, he would dig in after he and Bowie stood with Rose and Rhonda when they announced their departure from the hotel. Tomorrow would be the start of a new experiment for his friends Bowie and Rhonda and for himself and Rose. Bring it on, a bright new day.

# Chapter 27
# Confrontations

Rhonda stood at the window of the hotel room that had been her home with her sister, Rose. She watched the first pale orange streaks of dawn brighten the skies over city rooftops. She had not slept, anxious for this new day to begin. She whispered, "Rose. Roselita, are you awake?"

Her sister stretched and yawned. "Si, I am awake. So early. But I think I did not sleep a whole hour during the night."

Rhonda spoke, quietly. "We must go to the chapel. We must thank God for answering our prayers." She whirled, arms spread wide, full of excitement. "We must light twenty candles."

Rose threw back the bed sheet, sprang from the bed, and strode barefoot to stand with her twin. They embraced. Today they would begin a new life, uncertain where the unfamiliar path might lead, hopeful and confident in leaving the life they despised behind.

"Are you packed?" she asked.

"It will not take long, Rose. I will take enough clothing to get by, but I will leave most of it here. I don't want the smell of the johns to follow us. Maybe the next tenants can use it."

"Hurry then. Morgan and Bowie will be coming soon after we return from prayer."

"Yes, we must go now, but there is something I must tell you as soon as we return."

The two joyous women dressed quickly and almost ran to the chapel. They prayed for forgiveness for the life they led. They prayed to God and to the Virgin to watch over their parents and brothers and sisters. They prayed that the men they loved would love them too. They prayed for a brighter future. They lit twenty candles.

Bowie and Morgan waited at the hotel service entrance as agreed. Rhonda and Rose arrived, breathless from their walk and excitement. The foursome walked through the unlighted, vacant barroom, pausing to look at the booth where they had heard and gladly accepted Morgan's plan for the future. Jo-Jo would not start work until noon, guests and potential clients would not appear until late afternoon. Now, together, they would inform Grunwald of the women's permanent departure.

Rhonda took Rose's arm while the men continued ahead. "I must tell you something now. It's Bowie. I don't know what to do. He asked me to marry him when we were alone last night after you went to our room and Morgan went home." They stopped to face each other. "Rose, what should I do? We have been together, and I think I love him, but I am fearful too. You know how he can become so dark without warning, like another person."

"I am happy for you, sister. But we must talk about your fears when we can be alone. Later … not now."

Morgan called for them. "Come on, let's stick with our plan. Let's get this over with before he gets busy with morning checkouts."

Big John had watched the dawn from his hotel window, a grim smile on his disfigured face. He had often wondered what he might do if he ever encountered the slimy little shit that had robbed him and left him for dead. Now he had seen him. It was him alright in spite of the long hair and a line or two in the youthful face. It was him, and now he had a plan.

The text from Universal Services had said his tractor would be ready that afternoon. He would check out of his room and wait in his loaner vehicle near the service door behind the hotel until his target arrived. He would be there with a big surprise for the slimy sonofabitch. Then, he would drive off to get the tractor. No one would be the wiser—no way to connect him to his victim.

He took the elevator down to level G. The doors opened, and he stepped into the elevator alcove. He moved forward into the hall leading to the front desk. Wait! There the motherfucker stood just down the hall at the manager's office, him and his three friends from last night. That would complicate things. He took a step back. He pulled the 9mm automatic from his waistband. He waited and watched.

The foursome stood together confronting the red-faced manager. "You can't just quit!"

Bowie growled, "Watch us."

Rose added, "We are sorry, sir. It is something we must do now."

Then, the four smiling conspirators turned down the hall toward the Fiesta Room and the rear exit.

Big John stepped from the elevator hallway to confront them. "Not so fast, Sonny."

The four stopped just six feet from him.

"I don't expect you remember me, do you?"

Bowie stepped in front of Morgan and the women, fists balled, ready to defend or attack. The red, irate, eye-patched face conjured no memories. "Who do you mean? We don't know you."

"Well, Loser, you owe me about 5,700 American dollars plus interest. And a vintage Winchester rifle!"

What ghost was this? Bowie understood now. The trucker he'd killed a decade ago. He faced the ghost. "Big John."

"Correct on your first guess, Loser. And now it's payback time." He brought up the automatic and leveled it at Bowie's chest.

Morgan shoved Bowie away and stepped in front, raising his police badge in his left hand for Big John to see and reaching for his police automatic with his right. "Police. Lower your gun now!"

Big John instantly shifted his aim toward Morgan. "So, you want it, too?"

Bowie pushed Morgan aside, moving to attack their attacker. "Look out!"

Big John's three rapid shots hit Bowie in the chest. He staggered and dropped to his knees, then fell forward with his head on the floor.

Morgan's single shot tore into the big man's heart. He slumped and pitched face-down on the grimy hallway floor, lying head-to-head with his intended victim.

Rhonda screamed, "Bowieee!"

# Chapter 28
# Return to Reality

The *Mesa Star* ran the article on page four.
### Shooting at local hotel kills two.
Mr. Bowie Masters was shot and killed yesterday at the city's TruFont Hotel in an apparent daytime robbery. The shooter had registered at the hotel as John Smith. An off-duty detective from the Cactus Hills Police Department shot and killed the assailant on the spot. The detective, Morgan Morel, has been placed on inactive duty pending investigation.

Two hotel maids who asked not to be identified witnessed the shooting. Mr. Dean Grunwald, hotel manager, noted the maids were no longer hotel employees but were present to collect their severance pay.

Mr. Smith died at the scene. Mr. Masters was DOA at the hospital ER. Mesa police said they have not located any known relatives for either victim.

Aunt Esther read the notification from the Wisconsin Board of Bar Examiners to Morgan over the phone. "Your suspension from the bar for missing required CLE classes has been fully served and is now closed. In our final review of the matter, we acknowledge the suspension was imposed in error and was unwarranted due to your recent graduation from the Marquette University Law School and concurrent admission to the Wisconsin Bar. We regret our error and any inconvenience you might have experienced as a result."

Morgan entered the police captain's office to deliver his news. "Mac, my experience with you and the rinky-dink CHPD has taught me more than I learned in six years of law school. I will always be grateful."

Captain MacArthur stood and crossed his arms. "Okay, Morgan, let's have it. Ain't like you to not come right to the point."

Morgan continued, "It's time, Mac. It's time for me to return to the law practice I never started. I'm going back to Wisconsin as soon as you can see clear to let me go."

Mac nodded. "We knew it was coming soon. I have already made the decision that, when it did, I would fold up our tiny force. Harris and Aguilar both want to retire. We've been operating on a broken shoestring for years. We just can't make a go of it. I've told the others my plan. They have all lined up some possibilities."

Morgan offered, "I can stay a few weeks if it will help, Mac."

"No need to prolong the agony. The county is on alert to provide policing for Cactus Hills. Just leave your badge and weapon at the desk with Aguilar."

The two men shook hands. Then Morgan pulled Mac into a bear hug. "You're the best, Mac." He stepped back. "By the way, you and Denise are invited to a wedding Saturday at the little chapel in Mesa near the TruFont hotel. Ten AM. Very small and quick. No mass. No reception. No gifts."

"Denise wouldn't let us miss it. She told me you must be involved with someone. Anyone we know?"

"Not yet. I hope you both will get to know her some time. But we'll be packing up and heading north as soon as the padre says we are good to go. It's a long ride double on the Harley, so we'll take our time. Her name is Rose. Rose Rogers. Rose Morel after Saturday."

## Chapter 29
## Et cetera

The 130-year-old farmhouse in beautiful Door County, Wisconsin that Emile Morel had purchased when he retired in 2001 was feeling new life. Its five bedrooms, parlors, stairways, and kitchen felt the tread of young, unfamiliar feet on its pine-plank wood floors, and its walls echoed with the sound of new voices, cheerful voices, happy voices.

Julia Morel continued to visit her sister-in-law, Esther, at least six months of each year. Now, she had decided the old house needed a bright new façade. She applied a coat of bright white paint to the exterior walls and a deep sea-green contrasting color to the shutters and trim. Unable to safely scale the extension ladder, she hired two teenage boys from a neighboring farm to complete the second and garret floors.

She had plans for the interior, too, soothing pastels in a variety of hues. But that would have to wait until next year when she would return again from her long-time sanctuary on Buzzards' Bay in Massachusetts. This was the only family she had known all of her adult life—since that day when her nephew, Morgan, had contacted her about the death of her brother, Emile. She loved his wife, Esther, like a sister, the sister she never had.

Esther reciprocated the feeling. With Julia she had not been alone in the big house with only memories when Emile died. Her shop in nearby Fish Creek was closed these days, except for Fridays and weekends when tourists filled the streets. The quaint little boutique featured her own paintings along with works of other local artists—poets, sculptors, painters, writers, and various skilled artisans—woven goods, pottery, and jewelry.

Customers came to browse at leisure, perhaps first enjoying a cup of fresh coffee and Esther's legendary cherry-cranberry muffins. And they might have their charcoal portraits done in twenty-five minutes for $25 by Rose Morel, wife of her beloved nephew, Morgan—only five minutes and $5 extra for color-crayon highlights.

During the week, Esther and Julia were busy tending the three-year-old twins, Bowie and Vanessa, while their mother created the sketches she sold in her mother-in-law's shop and other of the hamlet's many retail outlets—landscapes of cedar, hemlock, or white pines forests, dairy farms and cattle, or cherry orchards in full bloom.

The twins were too much for any one person over the age of twenty, actively exploring the rooms of the old house, the chicken coop, the pond—running, always running from one short-lived attraction to the next, shouting and leaping into piles of autumn leaves their father had gathered for them, teasing the two aging women. There were quiet times, of course, when they napped—thank God—or sat captive listening to Dr. Seuss or the tales of Peter Rabbit, The Three Little Pigs, Jack and the Giant, Chicken Little, or such from the tattered pages of old nursery rhyme books.

Meanwhile, the children's father was busy preparing legal papers or giving financial advice at the Morel Agency in town. His skill in financial matters was apparently inherited from his uncle, not his father. The firm's success was derived from his detailed knowledge of the law combined with his empathy and concern for his clients' well-being. Old high school classmates helped establish the agency by word of mouth, and it quickly grew to be a valued resource for Door County residents.

Morgan watched his 11 o'clock appointment, Mrs. Robert Ashauer, enter the office exactly on time. He rose. She smiled, nervously running a hand through her short-cropped gray-tinged hair. He knew this woman now. He had known her as a girl forty pounds lighter and with flowing auburn hair. "Nancy, is that really you?"

"It's me, Morgan. Nancy Feldstein. Well, Nancy Ashauer for about the past 25 years. I …."

Her sentence hung unfinished as Morgan greeted her with a warm embrace and a kiss that lasted a little too long. Finally, flushed, she continued, "I was just visiting Dad on the farm. He is alone now and not doing well. I'm trying to get him to move into assisted living in Green Bay … near us. He's so stubborn. So, I was sorta in the neighborhood, and … well, we might need your help with his estate before long."

"Sorry to hear about your dad, Nancy. I'll be glad to help if and when you need me. Family rates, of course." Then he was conscious that they still stood—arms around each other. "Sorry, Nancy, please sit here. Tell me about you and your family."

The time had flown as they exchanged stories of their adult lives, still time enough for only the barest details. She learned of his life as a student, as a law officer, as an attorney, and as a husband and a father.

He learned her oldest child, a girl, was named Morgan and that Robert Ashauer taught high school in Green Bay. "You will never guess what he teaches, Morgan." She shook with laughter. "Physiology and hygiene!"

Ninety minutes later, she rose abruptly. "Look at the time! I really must go. Please don't get up." She patted his cheek, hurried to the door, turned, and put up a hand, smiling the smile he had always loved. "Bye for now."

Two thousand miles distant, Maria and Mateo Rodriguez were happy to have their daughter, Vanessa, back in their humble casa, even if just for a time. They knew their daughter, whom they must now call Rhonda, carried the deep grief of loss in her heart and a longing to return to the United States as an immigrant.

Every three months, Rhonda drove the aging family truck four hours from Islita to the American Consulate in Tijuana to check on her immigrant visa application progress. Each time, she returned desolate and dejected. The petition from her sister Rose, now a legal permanent resident of the States by virtue of marriage to Morgan Morel, was not yet successful.

"The waiting list is very long. Perhaps next time."

Rhonda searched for an affordable and suitable home for her parents. Both were still healthy, not yet plagued by one of the maladies that old age is almost certain to bring eventually. Yet, Mateo's back was bent and weak from years of toil in the reluctant Mexican soil, and Maria's eyesight was failing. Soon, they would not be able to care for the tiny casa that had been home to them and their brood for so many years.

Meanwhile, they prayed to the saints—Jude, Cajetan, and Anthony—for the miracle that the hopes of their daughter would soon be granted, even knowing when that happened, they would lose her again.

~~~

Stunned reading the letter from Douglas MacArthur, Morgan wiped his eyes before showing his two aunts the enclosed newspaper clippings. "Do you remember me telling you about my dear friends, Denise and Mac, in Arizona?"

"Of course, dear. You mentioned them often when we spoke. They seem like very good friends."

He read the news article first.

> Cactus Hills resident, Denise MacArthur was shot and killed in a failed bank robbery in Mesa yesterday afternoon. It appears she was an innocent bystander. The would-be robber, Mr. Weston Black, was immediately shot and killed by the bank guard, Douglas MacArthur, the victim's husband. Mr. Black, a long-time rodeo performer, was apparently homeless and indigent.

The enclosed obituary notice stated that Denise MacArthur was a retired school teacher.

> Mrs. MacArthur is survived by her husband and three small children, ten-year-old twins Danielle and David, and Daphne, the youngest. Denise loved daisies, the family noted, but in lieu of flowers, they request donations to St. Jude Children's Hospital or your favorite charity.

The last parents arrived to pick up their darlings from Mama's Place: Daycare for Potty-Trained and Preschool.

"Bye, Mama!"

"See you tomorrow, Mama."

"I love you, Mama."

Nora Masters checked the food-treats supply, *gotta keep the little bastards happy,* then turned off the lights and locked the door. It was a decent living if you could put up with the snotty noses and occasional dirty underpants. She could control most of the kids who parents brought to her for up to ten hours a day. There was a $50 surcharge if she had to stay overtime. There was plenty of demand for the service, and if any of the little monsters got out of hand too often, the parents were advised to find a new care center immediately.

Nora walked the few blocks to her apartment building. No need to pick up dinner tonight. There was leftover Chinese in the fridge. The setting sun bothered her eyes and did little to warm the chill autumn air. *Whatever became of Bowie,* she wondered, *he wasn't such a bad kid.*

## Acknowledgements

Too many to recognize have contributed without their knowing to my writing of this work of fiction. There are those whose paths have crossed mine in some small or large way, leaving impressions of appearance or attributes that have gone into shaping the essence of one or more characters in the story. There are family and friends who have expressed their support of the effort. Carrollton Writers Guild members have made innumerable and invaluable suggestions and corrections in addition to providing their continued encouragement.

One member of that group, author Stephanie Baldi, after hearing my short story based on one of the novel's characters, said "Oh, you must make that into a novel." After lying dormant and unattended for some seven or eight years, here it is finally. I am also indebted to Stephanie for sharing her detailed command of the English grammar and insightful queries into plot details during editing of the manuscript.

Author Helen Stine also read the completed manuscript. I am especially thankful for her astute perspectives on human emotions and behaviors, as well as suggestions for improved articulation and expression.

Elyse Wheeler, at Dancing Crows Press, contributed her great expertise in bringing the book finally into print.

I would be remiss to not acknowledge Dolly, my deceased wife of 66 years, the first reader of all my writings in the past. After each of my four books of poetry, an illustrated children's book and a collection of my short fiction were published, she remarked, "But, what about your book—you always told be you would write a book one day."

Here is your book, Dolly, a few years too late, but here it is at last. You made me do it.

Milton Keynes UK
Ingram Content Group UK Ltd.
UKHW020042210924
448622UK00011B/523